ALPHAS

TALES FROM THE AGE OF MONSTERS
BOOK'S 3 & 4

BY JOHN LEE SCHNEIDER

SEVEREDPRESS

ALPHAS

Copyright © 2023 by John Lee Schneider

WWW.SEVEREDPRESS.COM

ISBN: 978-1-922861-93-1

BOOK THREE: THE MAN WHO FELL TO EARTH

"Here am I sitting in a tin-can, far above the world..."
David Bowie

Timeline: This tale takes place between **KINGDOM OF MONSTERS** and **WORLD OF MONSTERS.**

CHAPTER 1

Where were *you* when the world ended?

When KT-day hit, some people saw it from the cities, some from the smaller towns, some were at sea.

One man saw it from space – and he saw it *all*.

Major Tom Corbett – call-sign '*Major Tom*'.

He was the Eye In The Sky, who had been in orbit for six months and was the only human being in space on KT-day.

A year later, he was finally coming home.

His lifeboat caught gravity as it dropped into the atmosphere, an escape-pod from the International Space Station.

Tom knew the world that waited below. He knew better than anyone, perhaps even Shanna herself, because the Eye In The Sky had files on *everyone*. He knew Shanna, he knew Professor Hinkle, Dr. Shrinker – he knew Monster Island.

And he knew Otto too.

Oh yeah, he knew *that* little bastard.

The Eye In The Sky capsule was ostensibly launched as an observation satellite, and Tom would agree that was an accurate statement, because it was enabling government observation of every satellite, cell-phone, camera, computer and database on the planet. Not actively *doing* it, mind you – just networking it so they *could*.

It had actually been good public relations for the EITS when Chinese space-debris hit the International Space Station, because Tom was able to pick up the ISS' duties when the onboard team was evacuated in lieu of repairs.

Those repairs were still on the to-do list when the world went and ended.

Tom had been left up in space all alone.

It was nineteen days before he finally received communication from below.

Tom always said the best way to eliminate the world-network would be some kind of super-virus. The pop-culture favorite, of course, was the EMP effect.

On KT-day, they got the virus. The EMP blasts came later, as if just to make sure the entire grid was completely wiped.

Still, that *should* have left Tom, up in orbit, mostly alone – he still had networking capabilities with the other orbiting satellites *and* the ISS.

But Tom's own system seemed to have been corrupted as well. More than that, it was as if some damned Gremlin had been running through his network.

As it turned out, there *was* – a quantum-Gremlin called Otto.

Among other things, the EITS had been inexplicably frequency-blind across multiple bandwidths, a condition that blinked on-and-off seemingly arbitrarily, leaving him periodically blind, deaf, *and* mute.

The life-support systems also showed signs of... not *failing*, so much, as simply randomly shutting-down.

From down on Earth, General Rhodes offered the cold comfort of duty.

Operating from orbit, Tom was still an asset, and Rhodes put him right to work, coordinating satellites, networking surviving missile silos.

Tom also found he could detect the accelerated energy signature of the infected giants, particularly in groups, and therefore where and when an outbreak was about to bloom.

So he stayed in space long enough to help save what was left of the human race – a very literal statement, because by ecological measure, in the year after KT-day, *Homo sapiens* had become a critically-endangered species.

From Tom's projections, it was still going to be close.

And after eighteen months, he was finally going to get a look at it from the ground.

Or die trying.

His orbit had at last taken him within range of the ISS. The EITS capsule wasn't equipped with escape-pods that would survive reentry, but the ISS was.

So today, after eighteen months in space, he finally fell back home to Earth.

He tapped his radio – he'd been broadcasting the same message since the moment he re-entered the atmosphere.

"This is Major Tom Corbett. Mayday. SOS. Anyone receiving my signal, please respond."

So far, no one had.

Tom looked out the window as the falling life-pod broke through the cloud cover and he could see open ocean below.

The Gulf of Mexico.

Not far, he thought, from the Yucatan Peninsula – the Chicxulub-site, impact-point of the KT-asteroid that brought an end to the Cretaceous, sixty-five million years ago.

The life-pod chute opened, breaking its fall.

Tom counted the seconds until they hit water.

CHAPTER 2

Tom felt the impact as the life-pod touched-down, plunging deep into the water. It was briefly dark again, before he bounced back up to the surface, bobbing like a buoy.

He'd landed. He was home.

Tom popped the hatch, looking out on the open ocean, and breathed his first fresh air in a year-and-a-half. He tasted the salt – it was heady, almost like a narcotic.

He sat for several minutes, shivering at the touch of both the sun and the wind, savoring as much as he could before he let pesky reality have its way with him.

Finally, he sat back into the pod, and tapped the screen on his console.

He wasn't out of the woods yet. Now, he had to get rescued. He'd activated every distress beacon he had available, but who knew how much tech still existed that could even read it?

That was to say nothing of anyone there to receive it.

ISS lifeboats were programmed to land more or less dead-center in the Gulf of Mexico, based on pre-KT-day scenarios, assuming a rescue coming from Houston. The Mount, however, was fourteen-hundred miles north.

With the slot-machine lights blinking on his console, Tom knew to count his blessings. He was happy to hit water and not a mountain, *and* on the right side of the planet.

But he was adrift in open ocean, he wasn't sure if his SOS had gotten through, *or* if there was anyone to come after him at all.

One year after KT-day, the Mount was the most significant single population of humans remaining on the planet, but Tom knew Rhodes had just suffered severe casualties, after the worst bloom of infected-giants since the first.

The Apocalypse did not *end* after KT-day – that was only the beginning. The rest came in cycles.

That was inherent in the nature of the Food of the Gods.

The military called them *'blooms'*, and they operated practically like random-firing, slow-motion nukes, capable of destroying entire regions. It was what happened when localized populations of the *'new wildlife'* became infected and spread, initiating a new cycle of madness, destruction, and death – a cycle that repeated as the infected beasts inevitably died, leaving mountains of infected carrion, all to be consumed, re-launching the infection, over and over, until it burned itself out.

For a time, Tom acted as sort of a 'bloom-spotter' from space. The military's strategy, under the scientific guidance of Dr. Anthony Shriver, was to nuke those sites before they spread.

Last tally, more nukes had been fired at these sites in the last year than were tested in all the twentieth-century.

This last big bloom was stopped just short of the Mount.

Tom stayed in the ISS long enough to see that. It had been the last thing he'd done for duty.

Now, he tapped his blinky computer, bringing up the last image he'd left on his screen – a woman named Kristie Morgan, his picture on the prison wall – he'd known her a year and they'd never met.

In fact, until he abruptly spoke into her ear a bare few days ago, she never even knew he existed.

First impressions were everything. In this case, it had been an anonymous voice from the sky that sent a chopper squadron to rescue her from packs of marauding sickle-claws.

Rhodes' team had gotten her out. At Tom's request. The General granted that one for *him*.

Tom looked at Kristie's picture on his blinky console. It was the only image he had of her. When the power went out, it would be gone forever.

Kristie was one of the early survivors. She had been living in a remote region of northern Alaska, and was already used to fending off the yearly migration of polar bears, so she was uniquely fortified.

This year, the bears were absent, probably already eaten, because the region was teeming with sickle-claws.

Kristie survived alone that first winter in her cabin. Tom knew because she had broadcast every day, transmitting radio and video – at first, calling for help – after a while, simply telling her story.

There was a lot of footage of her battles with the ravening sickle-claws, conflicts where she held her own, picking them off with a high-caliber hunting rifle. She could have probably endured indefinitely, but still needed supplies. Eventually, she'd abandoned the northern territory and began making her way south.

She'd actually made her way all the way to the Maelstrom military base in Montana – one of the last viable sites containing nuclear silos, and which General Rhodes believed up and running.

It turned out, however, all personnel had been dead for some time. When Kristie arrived, she found sickle-claws, not soldiers.

And of course, Otto.

In its way, it was serendipitous, because if she hadn't walked into that dromaeosaur-wasp-nest, no one would have known.

Everyone was lucky that day. Kristie was headed to the base's radio tower, before the clawed devils found her out, and she managed to make it behind the locked door before they mobbed her.

And as she radioed for help, trapped and surrounded, it also happened that Major Tom, after watching her for a year, trapped and mute from the EITS, had finally made it aboard the ISS, and picked-up on her signal.

He broadcast back directly to her radio, blaring from speakers practically right in her ear, calling her by name – he told her he was calling her from space.

"What the hell do you mean you're in space?" was Kristie's initial response. "And how the hell do you know my name?"

"My name is Major Tom Corbett," he told her. "I'm on the International Space Station, I've been picking up on your broadcasts for a year."

Sort of a stalker from space, Tom thought, wincing painfully at the sound of it.

"You've got help coming," he added quickly.

Rhodes, for his part, was as good as his word. Within minutes, the choppers were landing – and now they discovered how lucky *that* was.

The Maelstrom base was completely overrun. Besides the squads of sickle-claws, the troops found Otto in numbers, *crawling* over the missile silos, digging into the hardware like Gremlins – quantum-gremlins.

So yeah, that had been a good catch.

As for Kristie, Tom hadn't had the chance to talk to her since.

He couldn't blame her being dubious about having been watched from space.

On the other hand, Rhodes' choppers *had* arrived in the nick of time.

Tom was a Navy man, and not above playing the old *hero*-card if it helped win a lady.

It also didn't hurt that they secured the nuke-site and their *meet-cute* became a happy little happenstance that helped save the human race from final extinction.

At least, until the next time.

Tom sighed fatalistically, because he knew it wasn't ever going to really be over as long as Otto was still out there.

Otto did it.

So much came down to those three little words. You could pretty much point to any disaster anywhere. The little bastard had even infiltrated the International Space Station.

That had been a fun little discovery on his arrival.

At least it explained every damned thing that had gone wrong on his own capsule over the last year – they had interfaced the EITS network when he took over the ISS' duties.

There had been at least a half-dozen of the scaly little rats, maybe more. And while only two-feet tall, Otto's own sickle-claws could be quite formidable, especially in numbers – a troop of pissed-off saber-tooth house-cats in zero-gravity.

It had been a battle just to make the lifeboats. One of them followed Tom down the hatch, even as the ISS blew up behind them. He had crushed *that* little bastard with his bare hands – its broken corpse, still currently lay in the corner.

Otto's presence on the station should have been impossible. But that was how the scaly little rat *was*. He was small like a crow, out of sight and out of mind, but right there, underfoot.

He acted with a boldness that came from total lack of affectation or compunction – the way they exploited untouchable lands, in direct proximity to the largest cities in the world. In the United States alone, with over eighty-percent of land-mass uninhabited, many of the largest protected areas were actually *surrounding* almost every populated area in the country.

All the new wildlife really needed was a base-breeding population, and time to *grow,* using the government's own resources to keep it all secret and sequestered.

Otto was easy to underestimate.

To look at him, he was a miniature hybrid sickle-claw – scaly, with only hair-like quills instead of the plumage of its full-blooded dromaeosaur-relatives, giving him a naked-roadrunner/monitor-lizard appearance – another oddball *'glitch'.*

He talked in parroted-phrases, perfect mimics of human voices. And what one of them said, they *all* repeated.

And when they were hatched, they all said the same thing – in the voice of Nolan Hinkle himself:

"I am Otto."

Quite literally a mole, he had infiltrated every top-secret building in the country – likely the world – he apparently had the *run* of Area 51.

Otto managed to get into *space*, for God's sake. Tom would still be damned if he knew how the little sonofabitch did that.

It reminded him of something Shanna wrote in a memo to General Rhodes, just before KT-day.

After the incidents on Monster Island, it seemed she began to perceive Otto's true nature, although far too late to even guess the full scope of his machinations, or the looming threat.

Not that anything could have been done at that point – the 'bomb' was set and ticking.

Shanna's notes were brief, obviously understanding the hardheaded audience in General Rhodes, but she described her own empathy with the animals on her island – stronger with some than others, but completely absent in Otto.

Otto was an experiment in intelligence, but his reptilian brain hadn't yet evolved the capacity to *care.*

Without the corresponding bonding instincts, an intelligent reptile – or in this case, hybrid-dinosaurian proto-bird – just became a deadlier predator.

But while they lacked the ability to feel the softer emotions, they *did* share all those base-reptile urges and instincts.

As for what passed for empathy, that was harder to see, and only became apparent when a number of them were brought together.

One or two of them alone, they were nothing but scaly parrots.

But bring in number three, and suddenly their behavior changed.

Shanna never observed this on her island, because she only bred one at a time.

The jokers at Area 51 apparently just never paid attention.

And, in point of fact, might have been the largest enablers of the little bastard's extinction-agenda.

Shanna was vague in her memo, again catering to her audience, but she mentioned her *'id theory'* — the never-ending stream of nihilistic-consciousness that seemed to activate whenever Otto congregated in numbers.

"One of my father's areas of study," Shanna wrote, "was extinction-events. Doomsday-scenarios. It gave him nightmares. Sometimes, it would keep him up nights.

"I believe now," she continued, "Otto perhaps *was* empathic. He just hadn't evolved the ability to receive anything other than imagery, and base-reptile emotion.

"I wonder," she speculated, "if he was somehow picking up on my father's nightmares."

Tom, reading that passage as he sat trapped alone in space, months after KT-day, would not be the one to say this wasn't so.

He had been following the little lizard's path in the aftermath, tracing his activities, zooming-in with satellites, getting high-definition video of everything that was left down below.

The destruction seemed not just aimed at the human race, although that was a constant, but targeted at the very world itself.

Otto played with a lot of toys. Some of them were genetic. Some nuclear.

Some were seismic and geothermal.

Three weeks before KT-day, a volcanic eruption had sunk Monster Island.

Professor Nolan Hinkle died in the incident. Shanna herself only escaped through fortuitous circumstance.

Rhodes had sent Dr. Shrinker himself rattling Tom's cage over *that* one.

They wanted readings from every satellite in space, and every geometer on Earth, because that was a mountain that should *not* have blown-up. The genius who lived there *said* so.

After he collated the data, Tom's response was that it *wasn't* a natural eruption. Geothermal charges had been strategically placed to crack the volcanic cap.

Undeniable, deliberate and malicious intent.

But that was only a harbinger, because pretty soon the nukes started to fly.

And even given what *should* have been the sheer impossibility of an errant nuclear strike in the first place, it strained credibility that the missile that bulls-eyed the San Andreas Fault was just some random *whoopsie*, that finally triggered the long-awaited Big One and broke California off into the ocean.

Ripples of *that* one were felt throughout the continent. Geothermal activity awakened to levels not been seen since the *last* KT-extinction-event sixty-five-million-years ago.

The hit at San Andreas was twenty days after KT-day. In the months that followed, tremors along North America's volcanic ranges increased tenfold.

Otto, of course, took full advantage of that.

From what Tom could tell, the little lizard spent almost a year planting seismic charges at especially volatile spots all along the Rocky Mountain range, from Montana through Canada – just a little firecracker down the oil well.

Apparently, just for the sake of 'what's worse'.

When it was over, the upheaval nearly split the continent in two.

Tom had a great view of it from space – it was the last thing he'd seen before he fell from orbit.

It was also why his prospects for rescue were sketchy.

Tom was not sure if the Mount even survived. He'd made no contact since. And based on his blinky computer he was at least a hundred-miles from any land.

He considered his options.

Then the life-pod was bumped from below.

The craft was picked up and nearly capsized. Hurriedly, he shut the hatch, before water started pouring in.

After a moment, the pod bobbed upright again.

Tom looked out the window – it was right at the water-level, and he could see above and below the surface.

Up top, he saw the fin – better than six-feet high.

Below the waterline, he saw the shark – better than sixty-feet.
A Megalodon.

CHAPTER 3

Megalodons weren't just big – they were *scary*.

A sister-group to Great White sharks, they were a heavy-duty model – broader, more muscular, built to translate those 'Air-Jaws' Polaris-attacks on full-size whales.

Tom had seen infected-giants take out aircraft carriers.

This one was a 'normal', as the military designated non-infected individuals of the 'new-wildlife', but still likely weighed twenty-tons. Tom could see the six-and-a-half-inch teeth as it mouthed the life-pod, experimentally.

Tasting, Tom thought. Not biting hard – not yet – just seeing if it was something worth eating.

But then, after finding unappetizing metal, the giant shark released its grip.

With a final bump, the Meg turned away. The six-foot fin dropped below the surface, and Tom watched the massive beast disappear into the gloom.

Wasn't even worried, Tom thought.

He wondered what else might be circling around below. Hopefully, the Meg itself would frighten off other predators.

Although, as he looked out on the open ocean, all that *nothing* was really the greater existential threat. He had very limited supplies, and the life-pod had no means of propulsion, or even steering. He didn't even have a paddle.

There was a rubber life-raft, but... come on.

At the moment, it seemed he'd done everything proactive he could think of – a frustrating situation, because that left him with nothing to do but wait.

And float.

Just like in orbit – all this open space around him, but he was still sitting in a tin-can.

With the hot sun, he couldn't even ride up top – his skin was conditioned to starlight, and he would easily burn.

For a guy whose daily chores were life-sustaining functions, the next few days were excruciating.

The doldrums, they called it – no wind, just trapped in the stillness and isolation at sea.

On the third day, the life-pod's power sputtered and went out. The image of Kristie faded from his console.

Now he really *was* floating in a tin-can. All he had left was his hand-held radio.

He found the first giant's carcass on day five.

At first he thought it was a small island, a little blip of an atoll.

Then he realized it was an enormous, skeletonized corpse, floating on the surface.

It had once been an infected-sauropod. Tom estimated it was over a thousand-feet long.

A mountain of carrion – by the look of it, the ocean predators had been at it for at least a week.

There were probably a lot of these floating islands, Tom thought. Besides recent widespread blooms, the continent itself had just split in half, and would have dumped a lot of infected corpses directly into the Gulf.

Now the infection would pass on into the sea.

An *ocean-bloom*, Rhodes called it. From the Mount's perspective, they were like tidal waves, mostly out of sight, out of mind, but they rampaged across the oceans with every bit the destructive force as on land.

The first thing a bloom did was kill the indigenous scavengers that tried feeding on an infected carcass. The Food of the Gods was very quickly fatal to any non-engineered organism. It was a gruesome way to go, too. Professor Hinkle described it like an extreme allergic reaction at the cellular level – organisms would literally pop like bloated zits.

That left the new Mother Nature to take over.

Megalodon was far from the only monster in the sea – there was a whole menagerie of nightmarish creatures that far-outsized the largest predators to ever exist on land.

The giant, skeletonized carcass was at least a week old and, as he floated past, Tom could see some of the bites taken out of it were already pretty big. That meant infected-animals right in the region – the initial bloom had already started.

It was another two days later when he knew for sure it was going to be another bad one.

He had fallen into a half-dreaming stupor when he again felt the life-pod bumped from below.

Tom started awake, looking out the window to see yet another giant fin passing by.

This time there was no investigatory bite – just a quick bump and move-on.

As it moved past, Tom saw a second fin heading

the same direction.

And now a third – and several more behind that.

Megs didn't usually travel in groups – they were solitary like Great Whites. They only congregated...

Tom paused, frowning.

They only congregated around a large carcass.

Now Tom spotted the floating mass, barely a quarter-mile distant.

He squinted against the sun. It was big enough to be an island – floating carcasses, all infected-giants, clumped together.

Tom couldn't even guess the total tonnage. Many of these beasts approached a hundred-tons *before* being infected, so magnify that by a factor of ten?

He wondered how many animals. It reminded Tom of old fossilized boneyards, where dozens of animals had been found in riverbeds, buried together.

Some of them were already skeletonized.

But there were *so* many more.

And Tom was going to get a better look than he wanted. He had no way to steer the life-pod, and the current was drawing him uncomfortably close.

So far, these were all 'normals' circling. But these carcasses were more than a week old – the infection *had* to be spreading.

Even now, the scavengers were engorging themselves.

So far, most of the freeloading diners had been the Megalodons.

Then Tom felt his pod bumped and grabbed by the first of the late-arriving party-crashers, and his life-pod was pulled under the surface.

CHAPTER 4

The crocodile-like jaws that clamped onto the life-pod were over fourteen-feet long. For a moment, Tom worried their owner might simply try and bite through the craft, the way crocs did to turtle shells, but instead the pod was lifted and thrown, landing several yards away, splashing water, briefly sinking deep.

As the pod turned underwater, drifting back up to the surface, Tom looked out the window and saw the snaggle-toothed beast already sailing past.

The creature moved nimbly, its squat, compact body propelled by four seal-like flippers, trailing behind that massive *head*.

It was a pliosaur, a family of large, short-necked plesiosaurs – probably *Pliosaurus funkel*.

It was the one ocean-going sea-monster that could deal with Megalodon on its own terms.

In the modern post-apocalyptic ocean, it was the *other* alpha-predator.

Now, two of nature's ultimate monsters were sharing the same ocean, in the presence of *lots* of food.

So... would it be a pot-luck, come-one, come-all smorgasbord?

Or would it be a fight?

The answer was not long-coming.

Water exploded almost right next to the pod, as a sixty-foot Meg suddenly breached. The shark had two pliosaurs latched onto its pectoral fins. It thrashed in mid-air, trying to shake its attackers, before crashing back down, tossing the life-pod like flotsam with the cascading tidal-wave.

The ocean surface roiled as the battle erupted beneath.

As the life-pod bobbed below the waterline, Tom could see the pliosaurs moving in on the Megs, grabbing their fins and tails, with their barracuda-jaws, and then twisting like crocs.

Tom realized this wasn't a battle over the carrion – this was predation.

A pliosaur resembled nothing so much as a giant seal, and you didn't really see modern pinnipeds feeding on whale carcasses. They were active hunters of fish.

The pliosaurs were here for the Megs.

Their crocodile-like instinct to grab and twist duplicated the intelligent tactics Tom had seen orcas use on Great Whites – flipping the shark on its back, inducing tonic immobility, and the giant fish simply drowned.

Of course, the Megs did their own damage. Tom saw the floating remains of at least one pliosaur sporting a circular bite that took out its entire rib cage.

But for the most part, the other Megs, which were in much higher numbers, simply continued to feed.

Tom knew white sharks would cede territory to orcas, usually in response to predation. Did that instinct not exist in Megs? Or perhaps they viewed pliosaurs as rivals.

Or, Tom thought, as he watched the giant sharks engorge themselves on the floating, *infected* carrion, the real answer was in their eyes.

Their black, soulless shark-eyes were glowing emerald green.

Nolan Hinkle called it a glitch – an oddball side-effect of the Food of the Gods.

How long before this bloom of sea monsters fully blossomed?

The speed of the effect was directly related to consumption, and typically took days to weeks to fully manifest, depending on how much was ingested.

The intravenous effect was immediate.

Stuffed to the gills? Tom wasn't sure.

There were bites on those skeletonized carcasses that suggested infected animals were already experiencing growth. Even a big Meg had a bite radius of no more than seven-feet. Tom saw carved-out chasms significantly larger than that in *too* many of the floating cadavers.

Somewhere in the waters below, a bloom-cycle was already started.

First the beasts would grow. And once growth topped, that was when the mind began to addle, frying on chemicals a physical organism simply could not long contain.

Tom started the math in his head – how many carcasses, how many tons of meat, compounded by how many giant predators?

The numbers got scary pretty quick.

Although, 'scary' had become a relative term – Tom's little metal shell was batted past each individual skirmish, as twenty-ton super-predators clashed.

The current, at least, was finally starting to pull him away.

Tom glanced back – the battle was undecided, but the dynamic seemed established. The Megs couldn't easily get their teeth into the more maneuverable pliosaurs. And while the sharks were in far greater number, they were so preoccupied with their food-orgy most didn't even react to the pliosaurs until one of them took a bite out of their fins.

All of them – stuffed to the gills.

This was going to be a *big* bloom.

Even if the pliosaurs didn't eat the infected carcasses, the infection would spread secondhand when they went after the sharks.

Tom could see them under the surface – their eyes were all already glowing green.

Days or weeks, Tom thought, and this bloom would erupt across the Gulf like an underwater nuke.

He dearly hoped to be rescued by then.

CHAPTER 5

It was two weeks from his first touchdown that Tom saw the ship on the horizon.

His supplies were down to water and horse-pill-sized vitamin supplements that were hard to keep down. He had passed the *really-hungry* stage, and moved onto the part where his stomach simply hurt.

But he couldn't overdo the water – a challenge because of the heat. Despite himself, he'd already gotten a pretty good sunburn, just sitting on the capsule trying to escape the cooking oven inside.

Tom figured he had another week before he actively began to die.

After a year-and-a-half in space.

He was already growing weak. Just pushing the hatch open was a strain, and the effort of pulling himself up top left him out of breath. He was already badly atrophied from too much time in zero-gravity. Just moving at all was physical labor he was unused to.

The sunlight remained blinding after eighteen months of ambient light. As he bobbed on the life-pod, Tom squinted at the horizon, looking for the landmass that *had* to be there somewhere. The Gulf was landlocked on three sides.

Tom's eyes struggled to focus. He *thought* he saw an end to the horizon, the first possible shadow of distant shore, but it could as easily be a reflection on the waves.

He rubbed his eyes, as he leaned back, looking skyward, using the sun to log his direction. He'd been moving consistently south with the current.

Further from rescue.

Tom looked longingly back the way he'd come, and that was when he saw the ship approaching.

He blinked, slapping himself to full-attention.

It was still distant, but appeared to be a large vessel, at least the size of a Destroyer.

Had Rhodes gotten his SOS after all?

But Tom frowned. It actually didn't seem likely any potential rescue would come by boat. Nearly every naval-vessel, submarine or carrier had been destroyed. Travel by water was an extreme hazard these days. There were predators that could take out naval-craft *before* being infected with the Food of the Gods.

Primary among them were the Megs.

Tom had seen an infected Megalodon take a Destroyer completely clear of the water, breaching like a Great White hitting a seal.

There had been Megs about, and he knew an infection was spreading.

Now he saw the first evidence of it.

As the ship approached, it was led by a surrounding escort of fins, some of them better than sixty-feet high.

Tom also got a better look at the vessel itself. It wasn't military.

It *looked* like an oil-rig.

The Megs were not circling, but simply gliding alongside, leading, following – guarding all four corners, and likely circling below.

Atypical behavior for Megalodon. They didn't

school – they were solitary hunters, congregating only around food.

More importantly, they were fish. And normally, they *acted* like fish.

But when they started acting organized, the way they were now?

That put them into the odd category of beasts that seemed to fall under Otto's... you couldn't call it *'mind-control'*, exactly, because there was almost no mind in a Megalodon – it was *influence*.

It wasn't like Shanna, whose presence had a pacifying effect. Otto stimulated the primitive, reptilian-brain.

Otto, himself, couldn't even be truly said to have an IQ – he was a group-mind – it was like asking how much memory would the Internet have.

Tom wasn't even sure the little lizard truly concocted these nihilistic schemes or if they just simply proceeded, one step after another, like mindless marching brooms.

Their guardian Megs were even simpler. Already in constant motion, they needed just to be nudged and pointed – beyond that, it was impulse-stimulus, and it only had a few – circle, go deep, or attack.

Tom realized what this ship was – Rhodes called them 'death-ships', and you could recognize them by the fact they were on the ocean at all.

The sea was full of Megalodons, and Megs targeted whale-sized shadows on the surface. There could only be one reason this particular ship, within the target range of an infected Meg, was not being torn to pieces.

Tom knew what they would find onboard.

They were called *death-ships* because the crews of similar craft had been found slaughtered and eaten to the bone, and the boat itself overrun with sickle-claws.

And, of course, Otto.

Tom had seen those little bastards drive cars, pilot boats, fly planes, including fighter-jets — always three.

As the big oil-rig drew near, Tom could picture them in the pilot house, perhaps with the moldering corpses of the crew still strewn across the floor.

The boat was coming directly at him.

It was led by its escort of infected Megs.

Tom knew an investigatory-bite from an infected Megalodon would crush his lifeboat like a penny on a train track.

With no means of propulsion, Tom could do nothing but watch as the first of the giant fins turned in his direction.

But then it veered to the side. As did the next.

Tom popped the cap, cautiously peering out as the parade of Megs passed by — and now the three-hundred-foot boat bore down.

Was it coming for him? The Megs had deliberately parted.

Perhaps they wanted the capsule itself. Its power was out, but the computer still had its database.

Of course, they might just be going that way, and about to simply run right over him.

Either begged the question of what exactly was the little lizards' agenda today?

Tom looked back to the southern horizon, where the current had been taking him, leading into the Caribbean Sea.

And now, the mirage that he'd seen earlier was coming into clearer view – it was the first shadow of shore.

The shore of Mexico – the Yucatan peninsula.

Tom frowned, glancing back at the approaching ship – an oil-rig. Specifically, a drilling-rig.

What might be significant about this particular area to a quantum-level gremlin with a proclivity to seismic disruptions?

This was the south coast. They were right above the Chicxulub crater, impact-point of the KT-asteroid, that destroyed the world sixty-five million years ago.

A nuke down the San Andreas Fault had been enough to disrupt tectonic plates across half a continent.

What in *God's* name could that little bastard have in mind for the KT-site?

Not that it appeared Tom was going to live to find out.

The ship was indeed headed directly for him. Tom pulled down the hatch, bracing for impact.

But the boat was slowing down.

Watching through the window, Tom saw the big ship veer off-center, to avoid hitting the pod itself.

Now he could see sickle-claws, lined up along the railing like crows on a fence.

Tom's handheld radio barked static. He picked it up and heard his own voice talking back.

"This is Major Tom Corbett. Mayday. SOS."

Little *bastards*.

They *did* want the capsule. And Tom's own SOS was probably what alerted them it was there.

They had the tech to receive it.

Ah, irony, Tom sighed.

He looked down at the crushed remains of the single Otto he had killed with his bare hands.

God, he hated those scaly little rats.

He turned to the window, peering under the waterline, and saw the Megs were now circling as the boat drew to a stop. Their fins were poised and alert. Tom could see their glowing green eyes.

Waiting along the boat's railing, the sickle-claws were coiled like leopards on a tree-limb, waiting for Tom's lifeboat to come within reach.

He looked around for anything he could use as a weapon.

But then there was an eruption of water as the big ship itself was suddenly struck from below.

The lifeboat was tossed in its wake.

Tom saw massive crocodile-jaws rise up, engulfing the three-hundred-foot oil-rig like an antelope crossing a river.

The snaggle-toothed maw snapped shut.

There was an explosion, as the entire ship was crushed, bursting into flame.

Then the wreckage was pulled beneath the surface.

CHAPTER 6

Tom's life-pod was pulled down deep.

As he tumbled in its wake, he could see the giant pliosaur, its eyes glowing green, the ship in its jaws, twisting like a croc as it pulled the entire rig down.

It was not alone – several other massive seal-shapes circled in close, grabbing at the prize in their fellow's jaws.

Tom could also see flocks of sickle-claws scattering the ship like rats. The giant pliosaurs snapped at them as they swam for the surface.

No doubt Otto was among them.

That had to be why the pliosaurs were here. They were like tyrannosaurs that way – they *hated* those little bastards.

They also seemed to know when the scaly little rats were around, because they came after them.

That was why the escort of Megs.

Tom, however, had seen *T. rex* walk through fire and military munitions just to get at a single Otto, and it got worse with infected giants.

These pliosaurs were perfectly willing to go through Megalodons.

But there were a *lot* of Megs. It was difficult to measure sides, but just like at the island of infected carcasses, the pliosaurs were significantly outnumbered.

When the first of the Megs moved in, the pliosaurs initially evaded, parting to either side as the big shark charged past, jaws agape.

Deftly, one of them caught the Meg's tail.

The Meg turned sharply, lunging back with its teeth, but the second pliosaur grabbed its pectoral fin, and both giant reptiles twisted in the water, flipping the big Meg upside down, and into tonic shock.

Immediately, several other pliosaurs swarmed in and the shark was torn apart.

But now the rest of the circling Megs broke ranks.

Tom's life-pod finally bobbed back to the surface just as they began moving in.

Around him, the ocean began to roil.

Something hit his life-boat hard enough to knock him against the wall and nearly out. A second later he was hit again. He felt the life-pod tossed, and once more plunged deep beneath the surface.

After that, Tom wasn't sure exactly *what* happened.

He clung, bracing against repeated impact, as he was pummeled in a tempest of giants. He couldn't tell if he was at the surface or underwater — at times, he was in darkness, a hundred-feet below, and then he would suddenly be thrust back into daylight.

Tom wondered at what point the battered life-pod would simply break apart.

He knew he was actually lucky — the monsters were trying to kill each other. Killing him would just be incidental.

Tom thought of Kristie, whose picture had finally faded from his console when the life-boat's power died.

Then he was hit hard again, and felt the first spray of water, through the hatch. Several more heavy impacts followed in rapid succession.

Somewhere in the middle of that battering, Tom hit his head and the world went black.

CHAPTER 7

It was evening dusk when Tom woke up on a small atoll.

The ocean was calm. The life-pod had washed up on a sandy beach – a postcard of an island, perking up out of the ocean, with an outcropping of rocks and a bushy hairdo of trees and tropical brush.

Tom's body complained loudly as he rose, popping the hatch, and poked his head experimentally out into the salty air.

He was battered from head-to-toe. Shaken like dice in a cup, his arms and legs were mottled with bruises like leopard-spots. He found a nice goose-egg swollen-up where he'd struck his head.

But he was alive.

Groaning, he crawled out the top hatch, leaning his atrophied legs out over the side, practically falling into the ocean where the surf hit the sand.

The shallow water was tropical-warm. Tom felt his feet sink into the sand, the first time they'd touched the Earth in almost two years.

A wave struck him from behind, wavering him on his unsteady feet, and Tom staggered up onto the beach and collapsed onto the sand.

He lay for a moment just looking up at the dimming sky, trimmed in red, as the stars began to appear.

Red sky at night, sailor's delight. It meant the

storm had passed.

After a moment, Tom sat up, taking cautious steps, learning to walk again.

He pulled the life-pod to shore, and began rifling the remaining supplies – plastic water-bottles, flares, kerosene and matches.

There was also the small, handheld radio. He checked its batteries, and put it in his pack. Then he began gathering wood for a fire.

The little island was actually quite lush – the trees had coconuts and melons, and he found a tide-pool on the opposite bank full of good-sized crab.

With a fire going, he soon had himself set-up with a fairly decent banquet his first night back on solid Earth.

On the other hand, the island itself was barely a quarter-mile in circumference. The trees were stocked with maybe a couple weeks' worth of coconuts.

He spent some time fencing off the tide-pool, trapping the remaining crab, although based on the layout of the island, that might be a redundant effort. The pool was high in the rocks, indicating that, in weather, the majority of the island was getting washed over by the ocean.

The first decent storm and he would be carried back out to sea.

Tom squinted – he could *see* the mainland coast of Mexico was only a few miles distant.

But how to get there? The lifeboat left him adrift – he could be out for days, not to mention the possibility of simply floating on past the peninsula into the Caribbean Sea.

He supposed he could rig up some kind of sail

onto the lifeboat.

Of course, that left the question of what might be lurking in the waters between.

Not to mention what might be waiting on the mainland itself.

The thought of getting back out on the water was daunting. He had solid ground beneath his feet and, after drifting at sea, that was hard to turn away from.

He would give it a couple of days, he decided – regain his strength, stock up a little food. He had a little time.

With the fire crackling, Tom lay back on the beach, well-fed, his belly full of crab, melon, and coconut.

It could definitely be worse.

Tom shut his eyes and slept – he slept heavy.

He awoke to sun-glare coming from the east.

The ocean was calm, rolling the tide in like a morning walk. Tom sat up, wiping his eyes. His body was sore from physical exertion that just didn't exist in space, but it actually felt *good*.

He got up, stretched, looking out at the ocean.

Bits of flotsam were washing in – it looked like debris from the oil rig.

And just beyond the surf, Tom saw a large piece of wreckage coming in with the tide.

Riding on top, like an ice-flow, was a *pack* of sickle-claws.

Mounted on their backs and scurrying at their feet, was a whole troop of Ottos.

Tom could hear their chittering squawks carried on the warm morning surf, and then his own voice.

"This is Major Tom Corbett," it said. "Mayday. SOS."

CHAPTER 8

Tom looked around the beach for anything suitable as a weapon. Apart from a burning log and maybe a piece of driftwood, there was nothing.

Bare-handed against a dromaeosaur, he had no chance. Otto by himself could be a handful, and if those scythe-like claws on a two-foot rat gave you pause, the animals he saw rolling in on the morning tide ranged from jaguar to tiger-sized.

Tom almost laughed aloud at the thought of waving a flaming stick at a charging five-hundred-pound dromaeosaur.

His only chance was back into the lifeboat. Push it into the surf, and hope they couldn't get inside, or trap him on shore.

A troop of sickle-claws by themselves, and Tom wouldn't worry about that part, but with Otto?

Barely a hundred-yards out, the floating wreckage was bouncing past the surrounding reef. Tom counted a dozen full-sized sickle-claws, and at least that many Ottos.

They all stared at him eagerly, goggle-eyed, heads bobbing like hungry vultures.

Tom grabbed up his small handful of water-bottles and matches, along with a bucket of leftover crab-legs and ran for the life-pod.

Seeing him make his break, several sickle-claws jumped into the water and began kicking for shore. Tom was unhappy to see they were quite strong swimmers. As he tossed his minimal supplies into the life-pod, the first of them were already scrambling up onto the beach.

Tom tried to shove the life-pod into the surf, but it was stuck in the sand by the incoming tide, and Tom's muscles weren't what they were.

The sickle-claws' clawed feet bicycled in the sand like a cartoon as they came after him, hooting like screeching crows.

Cursing, Tom jumped into the pod, and pulled the hatch shut behind him.

A second later, he felt the impact as the dromaeosaurs all hit together.

The capsule was jolted in the sand, and might have been enough to knock it back into the surf, except there were now three five-hundred-pound animals perched on top of it, battening down.

Tom was startled at the ferocity of the assault – but that's how sickle-claws were – they *tore* at you, those powerful legs kicking like ninjas, disemboweling animals twice their size. The capsule rocked as those claws raked its surface, looking for a weak spot. Tom saw snarling jaws at the windows.

Forty-yards down the beach, the main wreckage washed ashore, and now the rest of the pack came charging over, with Otto scurrying among them, riding their shoulders.

For ten solid minutes they assaulted the life-pod – which was certainly scary as hell – but the craft held tight.

Finally, the sickle-claws backed off.

A shadow appeared at the window. Tom saw a trio of Ottos peering in.

"This is Major Tom Corbett," they said together. "Mayday. SOS."

Then he felt another impact – not a charge this time, but a push.

The larger sickle-claws were gathered to one side. There was another heave and the life-pod began to roll in the surf.

Inside, Tom held on as he was rolled along with it.

Were they pushing him adrift? He was fine with that.

Then he saw his bonfire. They were rolling him towards it.

Evidently, the idea was to cook him out.

That, Tom thought, might work. The life-pod itself was designed for reentry, but *he* wasn't.

This was better than waiting him out, in case he died, locked up inside, leaving them no access to the pod.

A boiling frog, on the other hand, will jump right out of the pot.

The lifeboat lurched as it was rolled up out of the water. Tom could hear the sickle-claws grunt like laborers as they wrestled the craft onto the sand.

Several Ottos bounced about the fire, tossing in branches and leaves, prepping it good and hot.

The same three remained perched at his window.

"Major Tom Corbett," they said together. "Mayday. SOS."

God, he *hated* those little bastards.

For a moment, he was tempted to just pop the hatch and take a swat at the scaly little rats with a wrench.

The larger sickle-claws would be on him in seconds, but at least he could take a few more of the little bastards with him.

Because he didn't think he was going to be able to wait them out.

At best, he was going to die suffocating in this pod, of heat or starvation, it was just a matter of when.

And with that, he grabbed up a large wrench, popped the hatch, and took a wide swing at the three Ottos perched at his window.

There was a loud roar, which Tom at first took for the wind, because he felt the blast of air.

But then he was distracted by the screech of all three Ottos coming at him with claws.

Tom timed his strikes, hatchet-style chops, catching each one as they leaped, their baby-scythe-claws outstretched, sending them broken and spinning like hard-hit foul-balls.

Behind him, the other Ottos hissed, and the sickle-claws responded instantaneously. In a blur of movement, they all came for him at once.

Then the roar of wind was broken by rotor-blades.

A moment later, it was machine-gun fire.

Tom ducked reflexively as the first of the sickle-claws mounted atop his life-pod were blown away.

A shadow appeared overhead as a military chopper circled, kicking up sand. Gunners on each side fired down at the mobbing dromaeosaurs.

Tom blinked, disbelievingly.

Someone got his message after all.

The gunfire lasted for several minutes, the pilot hovering a respectable thirty-feet above the beach. Tom approved – that meant an experienced pilot. Tigers in zoos leaped out of thirty-foot enclosures, and sickle-claws could manage at least that.

Tom also noted the gunners made sure to target every last scurrying Otto as they promptly abandoned their dromaeosaur cousins, breaking for the rocks and the brush.

When the beach was clear, and every one of the clawed devils, big and small, was shot-dead and twitching on the beach, the hovering chopper settled down and landed.

CHAPTER 9

The chopper blew sand as it touched down, and troops immediately filed out on both sides. There were a few single shots as they put down the last still-kicking sickle-claws, and another stray skittering Otto making a break for the brush.

Tom popped the hatch of the life-pod, looking at his first live human beings in eighteen months. He stumbled as he climbed out onto the sand.

The troops quickly surrounded him in a protective circle, and the leader stepped forward with a salute.

"Looks like we got here none too soon, sir," the soldier said. "My name's Hicks." He nodded to Tom. "You are Major Tom Corbett."

Tom nodded back, returning the salute.

"You got my SOS," he said, his voice croaking from disuse.

Hicks shook his head.

"Actually, we didn't," he said. "Other than your initial broadcast that you were abandoning the ISS, we didn't know if you'd even made it down. Or where. We were just searching the area where the space-station's life-pods are supposed to land."

Hicks nodded to the flotsam washing up on the beach.

"You're lucky, sir," he said. "We were close to giving up. But we just happened to spot that wreckage, and followed along a little longer."

"Rhodes sent you out looking for me?" Tom

asked, surprised.

"Well," Hicks said, glancing back at the chopper, "it was actually at the insistence of our passenger here."

Behind him, a young woman stepped out of the chopper.

Tom's breath hitched, and for just a second he actually thought he might swoon.

"The way Rhodes tells it," Hicks said, "she wouldn't leave him alone about it, so he finally sent us looking for you."

He stepped aside.

Kristie Morgan smiled.

"Major Tom, I presume," she said.

And for Tom, who had fallen out of space into a war of giant, rage-infected alpha sea-monsters, it was the most terrifying moment of his life.

He smiled back, extending his hand.

"It's good to meet you," he said.

Kristie's smile widened.

"Oh, come here, sailor," she said grabbing his hand and pulling him in close. "I've been waiting to meet you."

And with that, she planted a BIG kiss on him.

A whoop went up from the surrounding soldiers.

And Tom, a navy man, took the lady in his arms, and dipped her over, like in a waltz, and returned her kiss fully.

Somewhere behind them, someone snapped a picture – the new VJ-day.

Kristie was still smiling when Tom pulled her back to her feet.

"Nice to meet you," Tom said.

There was more hooting from the soldiers.

"Okay," Hicks said, "enough of that.

Everybody back onboard, and let's get the hell out of here."

Kristie took Tom's hand.

"Welcome back to Earth, Major," Kristie said. "Things have changed since you've been gone."

Tom nodded.

"I saw it on video," he said.

"Let's go, folks," Hicks cajoled, urging them onboard.

The troops boarded behind them, and the rotors kicked on. The chopper rose, turning north, the direction of the Mount, and left the little atoll behind.

CHAPTER 10

The sound of the chopper faded in the distance.

Far below, yet another piece of flotsam from the oil rig drifted with the current – just a small little chunk of railing.

A single Otto clung to it.

The little lizard had been adrift for almost two days and would probably have died soon, except that finally, *finally*, land stretched out ahead – the last branch of land in the Gulf, where the Yucatan peninsula bordered the Caribbean Sea.

Otto rode the piece of debris stoically, like a wounded gull, a scraggly, two-legged little lizard.

By himself, he wasn't much more than that.

But as the current took him towards land, other pieces of flotsam began washing together, and now he saw others, clinging like rats to broken pieces of hull, floating doors – one of them even had a life-raft.

All they needed was three.

They were now within the sight of land.

The Yucatan-site, the Chicxulub crater, was partially underwater. But it also stretched under the mainland.

It was believed that, sixty-five million years ago, an impact at this point destroyed the world.

The San Andreas fault was one thing. But there was no *end* to the possibilities here.

Otto chittered as the first of his kin was brought

in close with the current – the one with the life-raft. He hopped onboard, and the two chittered together.

The others were now coming together as they drew near land, some of them simply hopping off their floating debris and swimming, gathering aboard the raft like a flock of birds.

They were reaching the shallow water, when a massive shadow appeared from below.

The pliosaur was infected, although not yet fully-grown – but its glowing eyes were visible as it suddenly rose up, snapping the life-raft up in thirty-foot jaws. The giant reptile thrashed, tearing the boat to pieces, sending the scaly little lizards scrambling.

Deliberately, the pliosaur picked them off, one-by-one.

They didn't taste that good, and barely had any meat on them, but the big reptile was dutiful nonetheless.

It *hated* those little bastards.

The pliosaur rolled in the water, circling briefly, making sure it hadn't missed any.

Then it turned, heading back to deep water, and disappeared.

END of BOOK THREE

BOOK FOUR:
ALPHAS

"There's always someone bigger and badder than yourself."
Thom Jones

Timeline: This tale takes place after **WORLD OF MONSTERS.**

CHAPTER 1

There was something timeless about being at sea, Tom thought. Looking out on the careless ocean, it was hard to believe it had been twenty years since the end of the world.

Tom squinted as he peered out over the water, covering his eyes from the mid-morning sun.

The sea was as flat as gelatin, and the ship on the horizon came into view once again.

"Well," Tom said, "there he is."

The man beside him scowled.

"I'd hoped we'd lost him."

Mark Bakker was captain. Tom only met him a few months ago, on two other fishing-trips like today. The man's face once would have been boyish, but had grown cynical and hard, weathered from the cut of ocean wind.

Right now, Mark was none too happy about being there, and Tom couldn't blame him – the man had a pregnant wife at home.

It had been a decent day on the ocean until about two hours ago when they spotted the other vessel.

And Tom knew a death-ship when he saw one.

Just the fact of a strange boat being out this far was suspicious. Northwest Pacific waters were an aquarium full of the most dangerous predators in Earth history, almost exclusively, the biggest and baddest – Tom had done the reading, and that part had literally been *on*-purpose.

Any vessel braving waters like that had a reason not to care.

For the ship on the horizon, Tom had a good idea why.

He could imagine the smell, even from a distance – the stench of moldering, skeletonized corpses, gnawed clean by those disgusting little lizard-rats.

Otto. The little bastards would be there in numbers.

And they would no doubt be accompanied by their usual packs of guardian dromaeosaurs.

Mark's first-mate, a young guy named Pete, currently manning the wheelhouse, looked down dubiously.

"You sure about this, Cap?" he called down.

Mark waved him on.

"Keep on his tail," he called back. "But don't get too close."

Mark glanced at Tom, who nodded. Shanna asked them to *follow* – that didn't mean *catch*.

That was a fight they didn't want. Tom knew Mark was already edgy being out this far.

It didn't help when they saw their first Megalodon.

There was a murmur across the deck. The crew, ten men deep, including Mark, filed over to the railing, watching as the seven-foot dorsal fin sailed past. They could see the giant submarine-shape just below the surface.

"*Big* bastard," Lumpy the cook muttered. Beside him, Jimmy, barely eighteen, leaned forward fascinated, only to be pulled back by the two large fellows behind him. The Jonas brothers were old veterans, Big Jonas and Little Jonas – a separation, Tom assumed, that meant older/younger, because they were both quite stout.

The rest of the crew hung on the railing. Palmer and Wade were not much older than Jimmy. Russell and Perry were two more grizzled veterans. They all watched, until the giant shark dropped below the surface and out of sight.

"You don't usually see Megs around here," Lumpy called across the deck, to an affirmative group-murmur.

Mark gave Tom a knowing frown.

Megs were indeed rare off the Northwestern coast these days. There were a couple of direct reasons for this, but in the end, they both knew the first cause was simply, 'Shanna'.

Much of the dangerous new wildlife was more *congenial* in her presence – in fact, in her entire territory.

Megs were an exception.

Since KT-day, Tom had the opportunity to witness first-hand the predatory weapons of almost *all* of history's deadliest, most powerful super-predators.

The strongest, sheer bolt-cutter bite, would have to belong to the Devonian-era armored fish, Dunkleosteus. Pound-for-pound most destructive was *T. rex*.

But for total, unequivocal, biggest predatory-hit nature ever designed? That was Megalodon.

Megs were actually designed a bit *like T. rex* – stocky and torpedo-like, built to hit fast and hard, with a devastating first strike. Megalodon was a shark that targeted whales.

Or in modern days, comparably-sized boats. And infected giants could be six-hundred-feet long.

From the vantage of the wheelhouse, Pete scanned the horizon, covering his eyes.

"You think there are any more of them around?"

There was another uneasy murmur across the deck.

"It might not hurt," Mark said, "to take a look and see what's down there."

He nodded to Tom, who followed him up top. Taking over for Pete at the wheel, Mark tapped the screen mounted above.

The sonar equipment was Shanna's IQ at work, reintroducing modern tech to a post-apocalyptic world. Although, in the case of Shanna, it was usually an upgrade.

Mark's sonar device was one example – intended as a fish-finder, solar-powered, made from melted plastic, randomly collected, as the ocean pushed generations of human clutter back on shore.

It also functioned as an alert for anything large enough to threaten the ship.

The alarm was beeping now.

Mark's boat was the biggest in the fleet, handpicked and refitted from a choice of abandoned old-world vessels, even an adult Meg wouldn't be able to sink it.

Most likely.

Of course, a really *big* shark might be able to disable it – or perhaps more than one.

"What have you got?" Tom asked, looking down at the beeping screen.

"Megs," Mark replied unhappily, "we've got Megs."

He frowned, looking at the screen.

"Among other things."

The screen showed several large blips within the immediate vicinity. At least three other Megalodons were perusing the area. But the sonar also showed several less-distinct images, at a wider range.

"What is that?" Tom asked.

"I don't know," Mark said. "Something moving in a group."

He looked up, nervously.

"A *lot* of somethings."

Tom said nothing. When Shanna asked them to follow the death-ship, Mark took some convincing, objecting on the grounds that it was too dangerous. Mark was pointedly *not* reminding Tom of that now.

There was no need – he knew Mark wasn't wrong.

After all, Tom had gotten a better look at Armageddon than anyone – or at least a more comprehensive one.

It was actually freeing to talk about it, now that all that top-secret stuff was over. When they first met, two fishing-trips ago, Mark asked the perennial question among old-timers, 'where were you *on KT-day?'*.

"I was up in space," Tom replied easily, "sitting in a non-spy capsule that just happened to be hooked into every online-device and cell-phone on the planet."

That raised Mark's brows – one he hadn't heard before.

"Then," Tom continued, "after being stuck up there for a year, with three-hundred square-feet of living space, they dragged me off to the Mount to live in a cave."

Tom smiled, indicating the surrounding ocean.

"I tend to like wide-open spaces these days."

Mark had shrugged.

"Could be worse," he allowed.

Tom caught the tone.

"You don't like fishing?"

Mark smiled.

"Gets to be pretty hard work, day-to-day. But someone's got to. And what else is there to do on the coast? Logging's worse."

"Why not live in the Valley?"

"Because there's a two-hundred-foot *T. rex* named Junior that doesn't like me much."

That raised Tom's own brows.

"I shot its mother," Mark explained. "*T. rex* hold grudges."

Tom nodded.

"I've heard of things like that happening."

"You lived on the Mount, right?" Mark said. "Yeah. You heard about *this* one. From a young lady named Lily, I'll bet. Or one of her friends."

"It was in fact," Tom said, "a young lady named Sabrina. Her mother was named Lily."

"Mother?" Mark frowned.

"It sounds like we know some of the same people," Tom said.

Mark nodded.

"When you booked this charter, my wife said she knew you from the Mount."

Mark smiled a little.

"Sally's a little claustrophobic too," he said. "But she's worse about boats."

Tom nodded. He'd heard that story too – he

had known Sally at the Mount.

In point of fact, Sally Crawford was General Rhodes' personal assistant and a person of some stature. As it followed, Tom knew a little of Mark's own story before he did.

Living on the Mount, Sally raised a daughter. Dawn was one of a handful of children growing up in the new world – part of the *Arc Project*. Sally rarely spoke of Dawn's absent father, but her official line was that he was dead.

Tom knew better. Because she *pined*. And you don't pine unless someone's still out there.

They were not reunited until the Mount fell, less than a year ago, after Mark thought her twenty years dead and gone.

He also met his daughter, now eighteen.

And now with another on the way, Mark did not want to be taking risks today.

Tom sympathized. He had a lady back home himself.

He regarded the disturbingly large blips on the sonar screen.

Shanna would understand if they turned back.

There was a louder beep as that odd, indistinct signal was now registering closer.

A *lot* of something.

"Hey, boss," Pete said, looking out the window, "you gotta get a look at this."

Tom and Mark both turned. Tom was expecting to see six-foot fins, and wasn't disappointed.

But these weren't the triangle shark-fins of Megalodon – these were tall, and slender.

And black.

Blackfish.

It was a pod of orcas.

CHAPTER 2

It was a *big* pod of orcas, perhaps two-hundred or more. Tom had never seen them in the wild.

"They've been around lately," Mark said. "I've gotten the word from a lot of other fishermen too."

Outside, the crew was whistling as the pod circled their boat.

Tom knew enough about orcas to recognize a diverse group, and understand that was unusual. He counted at least three different eco-types based on their fins and markings. Ecotypes normally didn't mix.

Of course, that was the old-world. Orcas were nothing if not adaptive. Tom was actually surprised they were still out there at all, considering the denizens of the post-KT-day oceans.

"They aren't called killer whales for nothing," Mark said. "They're big, powerful animals. But more than that, they're smart. *Very* smart. Hominid-level intelligence. And they compete just fine.

"But," Mark allowed, "you don't usually see them around *here*."

"Why is that?" Tom asked.

"The same reason," Mark replied, "you don't see Megs."

Tom nodded. That specific reason was pliosaurs.

This was a direct effect of Shanna's influence.

Pliosaurs were big, Megalodon-sized reptiles, with seal-bodies and crocodile-jaws. Scientists once called them the *T. rex* of the ocean, and for whatever reason, despite a much more primitive reptilian-brain, the big pliosaurs responded similarly to Shanna.

That was the reason fishing was possible off the northwest coast – pliosaurs, drawn by Shanna's pacifying influence, drove out other competing predators, including the much less-congenial Megs.

And even though, like *T. rex* itself, *outside* Shanna's influence, they could be much less pacified, pliosaurs were fish-eaters, not typically inclined to attack large boats on the surface like Megs were.

They did, however, present a problem for orcas. Their maneuverability was comparable to the orcas' own, and they were specifically evolved to catch fish roughly twenty-to-thirty feet. Their fourteen-foot jaws whipping to either side, off a thick, broad neck, could kill a twenty-five-foot killer whale at a stroke.

Faced with a rival predator that trumped their own strengths, the intelligent orcas took the prudent course of simply avoiding the territory, keeping north, or to the deeper, colder waters further offshore.

But they were here today.

The crew watched as the orcas circled, some sky-hopping as they passed, others waved their tails.

"They're sure trying to get our attention," Tom said. "Did Timmy fall down the well?"

"Or," Mark returned, "are they warning us back?"

He pursed his lips in a piercing whistle. Outside, the crew jumped to attention.

"Get out there," Mark said to Pete. "Everybody back at their stations. We might be leaving soon."

"Yes, sir," Pete responded, turning for the stairs.

Out on deck, young Jimmy was leaning over the railing, fascinated, as the harlequin black-and-white shapes porpoised past.

"What are they doing?" he said, as Pete pushed him back from the railing.

Mark glanced doubtfully at Tom, shaking his head.

"Orcas *and* Megs. On the same day. And a friggin' death-ship?"

"Yeah," Tom replied, nodding. "Probably coincidence. Nothing to see here."

Mark groaned, clearly not wanting to see any more.

The presence of Megs, especially in numbers, was telling by itself. Mega-tooth sharks *never* encroached on pliosaur-territory. There was only one reason they would.

Otto.

Tom ground his teeth. The little lizard was like a cancer, always just waiting to metastasize somewhere.

"Little bastard," Shanna had muttered when they radioed in an hour ago, after spotting the errant ship.

"We knew he was still out there," she said, rueful and resigned. "Therefore, he was up to something."

Tom knew that painfully well.

"But," Shanna allowed, "maybe this time we can get ahead of it."

"You want us to chase him down?" Tom asked.

"*Follow*," Shanna said. "See if you can get an idea of what he's up to."

"I don't much like the thought of following a death-ship out to sea," Mark interjected. "We're pretty far out if we get in trouble."

Shanna gave Mark no out.

"It's up to you," she said, "if you think it's too dangerous, I trust your judgment."

"For the record," Mark replied, "I think it's too dangerous."

Then, disgruntled:

"But we'll follow. For a while. But I ain't gonna smile."

"Keep in touch," Shanna said.

That was an hour ago.

Since then, they'd seen one Meg and counted four more on sonar. Tom wondered how many more were out there.

He wondered if they were avoiding the orcas.

Or possibly dropping down deep to target surface prey?

That question was answered a moment later when the fishing boat was hit from below with an impact like a surfacing submarine.

There was a collective grunt from the crew as every hand latched onto the nearest rigging. Jimmy almost fell overboard, but Big Jonas caught the scruff of his shirt, only to slip himself – Russell and Lumpy pulled them both back in a jerk.

Tom and Mark braced against the walls of the boathouse as the boat settled.

"*That*," Mark said definitively, "was a Meg."

And sure enough, a seven-foot fin had risen up just next to the boat.

Five Megs, Tom thought. At *least* five.

How many hits would it take to incapacitate their two-hundred-foot boat? Or even sink them? They were a long way out to sea.

Mark shook his head.

"That's it. We're out of here. A hit like that on the motor and we're stuck." Mark shook his head. "Best case scenario after that is Maverick picks us up in his chopper. You want that?"

Tom cringed. They'd both flown with Maverick, and vowed never again.

"But," Mark said, eying the Meg-fin keeping pace beside them, "we still have to *get* back."

The Meg showed no signs of backing away.

There *were*, however, roughly two-hundred orcas, who took umbrage at the sudden intrusion of a giant mega-tooth shark in their midst.

Tom had seen old-world footage of orcas killing Great Whites by flipping them on their backs, inducing tonic mobility. With a Meg, it was more like how they went after big whales – they came in mobbing and battering, slamming into its belly and gills in rapid succession and then retreating.

A collective whistle sounded from the crew as the Meg reared dramatically, showing its teeth, lunging after its smaller, faster attackers.

The orcas fell back, letting the shark expend its energy before moving in again. This time a pair of them latched onto one of the pectoral fins – this was where they would flip it over.

But the giant shark jerked away, sounding, and diving deep.

For long minutes, there was nothing. Then the Meg's fin reappeared further out, giving the orcas distance.

The pod circled back in front of the ship.

Out on deck, Jimmy looked up at the boat-house.

"Are they... *protecting* us?"

Mark glanced at Tom, who was likewise at a loss.

The Meg continued to circle at a respectful distance.

Then another shark's fin rose up beside it, this one even bigger.

And then another.

Mark's sonar beeped. Now there were several large blips on-screen.

A *lot* more than five.

Tom saw the first of the circling fins turn, veering in towards the boat.

And in the water just outside the boat, their supposed line-of-defense, the orca pod, abruptly sounded and was gone.

"Well," Tom said, "so much for *that*. I guess they didn't like the odds."

"Yeah," Mark agreed. "Neither do I."

The lead Meg-fin was arrowing towards them – the others turned to follow.

On the console, the sonar-warning beeped.

There was generalized garbled cursing as the crew braced for impact.

But the hit never came. As the Meg closed, it was struck from below by something just as large.

Tom saw elongated, snaggle-toothed reptilian jaws clamp onto the shark's already-damaged pectoral fin.

"Pliosaurs," Mark said. "That's why the orcas left."

He nodded confidently to Tom.

"The Megs tend to get the worst of these."

Tom, who'd seen it up-close and ringside back in the Gulf of Mexico, tended to agree. Megalodon packed the most powerful, most devastating strike ever, but the biggest hit didn't always translate to how well you paired against another predator.

With Megs versus pliosaurs, it was a single-strike attack from the shark pitted against the seal-like maneuverability of the pliosaur.

For the Meg, being grabbed by the fin was often enough to end it – the pliosaur's reptilian instincts duplicated the intelligent tactics of orcas killing Great Whites, latching on to the shark's fins and twisting in a crocodilian death-roll, flipping the Meg on its back.

But remarkably, *this* shark reacted as if it knew the attack was coming. It suddenly jerked to one side, teeth extending from its jaws, ready to strike. The nimble pliosaur, however, still caught the shark's injured peck-fin, clamping down with snaggle-teeth and twisting, ripping the fin loose.

The Meg jerked away, clearly in distress, and the pliosaur grabbed onto the tail. In a quick, deft, full-body twist, learned or instinctual, it flipped the shark onto its back. The Meg went paralyzed and still.

Mark's sonar continued to beep. Several more large shapes circled below. But up top, the rest of the Meg fins veered off again, dropping below the surface and out of sight.

Beside the boat, the pliosaur remained at the surface, the immobile, drowning Meg still latched in its jaws.

Mark steered the boat respectfully back. It was

Shanna's influence, after all, that pacified these big reptilian predators. They were a long way out, and nobody there was Shanna.

Then the pliosaur also sounded, passing under the fishing boat as it disappeared into the deeper waters.

The sonar continued to beep. A *lot* of something large was still prowling about below.

But out on the horizon, the death-ship was gone.

CHAPTER 3

Shanna was waiting on word from Mark and Tom when she heard the approaching footsteps of a giant.

She'd learned to be wary of that sort of thing, ever since a thousand-foot brachiosaur stepped on her house – a cozy, lakeside home where she'd lived half her life.

It had almost stepped on her husband too, as Cameron would remind her.

The *new* house was built on the same lot, albeit to Shanna's new construction standards – basically, a low-budget version of the house her father built back on the island.

Not that Shanna hoped to test it, but the new structure actually *should* be able to support a single step of an infected sauropod.

She went to the window to see what was coming their way today.

Standing on the ridge, rearing up above the trees, its head rising over two-hundred-feet, was a giant *Tyrannosaurus rex*.

This particular beast was well-known in the Valley, called '*Big Red*' for the red-tint to his skin, but it also fit his pugnacious nature – a product of having once been an ostracized hatchling, picked-on and nearly killed by his siblings.

Now, as far as Shanna knew, he was the biggest rex in the Valley and the most powerful, most terrifying creature on the continent.

Riding on his shoulders, tiny as a pigeon on a city-bus, was a young man named Lucas, who was also well known – predominately as the only one, besides Shanna herself, who could actually *ride* a rex.

Shanna called into the living room after her daughter.

"Leanne! Your husband's home."

When Shanna first came to the Valley, she had only just become pregnant. Now Leanne was within weeks of making her a grandmother.

Leanne was just one of a whole troop of expectant mothers in the Valley, introducing a second-generation into the new world.

The old world was becoming nothing but stories and memories – a world Shanna, having grown-up so isolated, hadn't known all that well herself.

Of course, Cameron was there to remind her. He and his crazy pilot-friend, Maverick, along with Major Tom and most of the older settlers, were constantly comparing the world then to what it was now.

Cameron described the Valley as the *Flintstones* meet the *Jetsons*. With a bit of *Little House on the Prairie.*

Shanna's tech actually provided quite modern conveniences – electricity, refrigeration, and heat, all with no need for public utility – just small, individual generators – something that went a long way to preserve the rustic settings.

Leanne grunted, hefting her third-trimester weight off the couch, and joined Shanna at the window.

Big Red thundered to a stop behind the house.

Lucas let out a piercing whistle and the giant

rex kneeled like a steed, lowering his head, allowing him to dismount.

Shanna and Leanne went outside to meet them. Leanne, waddling with her belly full and round, greeted Lucas with a hug and wet smooch. Shanna smiled, even though she could tell Lucas was worried.

Big Red reclined on his haunches in a duck-like resting pose, his massive head settled regally between his shoulders.

"I took him out for a run," Lucas said, patting the stone-leather hide. "He's been a little edgy."

Shanna nodded.

"Me too, actually," she said, and Lucas frowned. Like everyone in the Valley, he'd learned to heed Shanna's moods.

For her part, Shanna listened to Lucas about *T. rex* – he'd been riding them since he was a kid.

Big Red, in particular, responded to him like a pet dog. As a boy, Lucas raised him from a hatchling, after finding him with a broken-leg – a gift from his siblings, over his red-skin. Lucas nursed the little creature back to health and the two were inseparable to this day.

Now the giant *rex*' breath rumbled out in a low growl. Shanna could see Lucas was right – Big Red's hackles *were* up.

One wondered *what* might make a two-hundred-foot Tyrannosaurus nervous?

Shanna considered. Mark and Tom *had* called in a death-ship.

Otto was always a good start.

Big Red's eyes were slitted like a wary cat's in pretense of sleep.

Once upon a time, a giant like this would have meant an infected, rampaging monster, but the big rex was missing the tell-tale glowing green eyes.

Big Red was exposed to the Food of the Gods in the last big bloom – more of Otto's continuing nihilistic efforts – but infection was no longer a death-sentence. Shanna had developed a cure.

Not a *'cure'*, exactly, because the growth was permanent, but rather an antidote that neutralized the chemical before it progressed into the final stage of madness and agonizing death. Shanna described it as sort of a super-analgesic.

So now, infected-animals didn't have to die, and you didn't have rampaging giants. The infection would also no longer be passed on through consumption.

Of course, the antidote had to be administered.

There was also the problem of what to *do* with these surviving giants.

In the case of Big Red and the Valley's pack of *T. rex*, they became extremely formidable guard-dogs.

Lucas was their keeper and even Shanna was impressed over his way with them.

But the *T. rex* were edgy lately. Shanna sensed it too.

"It's *all* of them," Lucas said. "They're upset. They're sensing something they don't like."

They all had a pretty good idea what *that* meant.

"Otto?" Leanne said, looking back at her mother. "So soon?"

Shanna nodded.

"The little bastard never sleeps."

Mark and Tom's death-ship was confirmation enough the little lizards were about. But was that really what Big Red and the rex-pack were sensing? All the way out at sea?

Or were they skulking about the Valley somewhere? Maybe just beyond its borders?

That might seem foolish – the *T. rex hated* Otto, and would sniff them right out – root them up like bears clawing termites out of a log. *Always.* There was no hiding from that tyrannosaur-nose.

But that was the thing – their nihilism was total. Personal-survival was not a factor. They demonstrated that clearly after their last debacle, when they were nearly wiped-out themselves.

Shanna wondered how ideas manifested in their gestalt-mind. They weren't creative – individually, they were like drones, activated by their collective group-think.

Their efforts at problem-solving were a case-study all on their own – unerringly, maximizingly destructive, as if sabotage was so ingrained in their genetics they couldn't *not* do it.

T. rex, for example, like Big Red, were one of their most persistent antagonists, but their original KT-day-coupe created a giant rampaging *army* of tyrannosaurs looking to stamp *Otto* out as much as the rest of the world.

And evidently, the lizard's group-think finally decided the way to go was more hybridization – in this case, Otto's own DNA spliced with tyrannosaur-eggs stolen from Big Red's first brood.

That one, Shanna thought tiredly, hadn't worked out so well.

The offspring was... rebellious.

It called itself '*Draco*' – picking up the satiric moniker '*Dragon Lord*', along the way – a dromaeosaur-clawed tyrannosaur, with a quantum-level IQ, who didn't much like humans or mammals in general, and was mostly dedicated to wiping humankind off the planet.

Funny thing though, he inherited his *T. rex*-loathing of Otto, as well – and, in fact, had wiped most of them off the continent.

Otto often demonstrated the collective ability to induce embolisms in creatures under his influence – painful mind-zaps, that grew more potent with his numbers, and at one time, been able to drop Shanna herself in her tracks.

But Draco was on another level – once he and Otto fell to squabbling, Draco simply fired back.

At this point, Draco had become infected with the Food of the Gods, himself, and his own end was nigh. But in his short reign, he left a very different world behind, even from the post-apocalypse that it *had* been.

One could make the argument the change was for the better.

The Mount was gone, and its survivors relocated to the Valley.

And without Draco, Shanna never would have been forced to finally create the antidote for the Food of the Gods.

That was not to mention nearly wiping Otto off the continent.

Draco's single mind-zap wouldn't have killed *all* of them. The scaly little rats were everywhere – Tom told her they'd even managed to get into space – but Shanna had not felt that odd presence, that sulfurous psychic *stench*, since the Dragon Lord fell.

But in the last several months, the little lizard had clearly been regrouping.

Big Red's hackles were up.

Of course, that was, at least in part, because *he* was among the Valley's expectant fathers.

One of the things the Dragon Lord left behind was a world full of giants. Big Red's mate was originally selected by Draco as his own bride – and in fact, she was the test-subject for Shanna's antidote – a coerced experiment, with Draco breathing over Shanna's shoulder.

But the antidote worked, and when the war was won, and Draco was gone, the giant rex-queen – Shanna nicknamed her 'Queenie' – came back with them to the Valley.

Queenie more or less inherited leadership of the local pack of females – a rough-troop in their own right. Black Beauty was the largest, Rosie was her little sister. Tink – 'Tinkerbell' – was the youngest. Then there was Lizzie, after Lizzie Borden, a nod to the big female's temperament.

A formidable entourage, but Queenie assumed dominance as if it were hers by right.

And despite a rocky start, she and Big Red seemed to hit it off.

Her brood was due soon. Shanna wasn't sure what effect the Food of the Gods would have on the rex' pregnancy cycle, so it could be days or weeks.

In fact, it was a sort of race to see which of the Valley's expectant mothers would deliver first.

Based on presumed moment of conception, Shanna's best friend, Rosa, should be the odds-on favorite, a gift from Cameron's friend, Maverick. Rosa, who was also the town doctor and midwifed Shanna's pregnancy, placed her own due-date first.

Then there was Sally, reunited with Mark after eighteen years, and already presenting a nearly-grown daughter, she was now only a few weeks away from giving him another.

There were a few other candidates among the new settlers, but Shanna, personally, thought it was going to be Leanne.

Her daughter was always in a hurry.

Shanna was also getting one of her... hunches.

They were getting stronger these days.

She was pretty sure Leanne felt it too. Her daughter had been acting spacey since she entered her third-term.

Shanna's third-trimester was when her... perceptions... really seemed to come alive.

Leanne herself hadn't quite realized it yet, but it was more than just the glow of motherhood. The empathic light that joined them was growing stronger.

Shanna had no idea what that meant down the line – they were all in uncharted waters.

Between that and a nesting two-hundred-foot female Tyrannosaurus, there were more than just the typical problems of dealing with a lot of pregnant wives.

After the Dragon Lord's war, the Valley was still in a time of recovery, and needed time to heal.

The *last* thing they needed right now was Otto – *anything* to do with Otto.

But the little bastard was malingering about somewhere.

Shanna looked up at the sun, moving too quickly across the sky.

They hadn't heard from Mark and Tom in over an hour.

Shanna glanced up at Big Red, and heard the low rumble deep in his throat – the big rex remained agitated.

On the strength of that alone, Shanna was too.

CHAPTER 4

The thing about Otto was that you had to think worst-case scenario. You also had to recognize he was never going to stop.

What *this* time? Shanna was afraid to imagine.

In the past, it had been seismic disruptions, nuclear missiles, on top of the widespread distribution of giant, rampaging monsters, via the Food of the Gods.

They needed a new one. Now that an antidote existed, Shanna could stop a bloom.

Otto wasn't creative. His ideas were few and far between, and he could only enact one nightmare at a time. That was both good *and* bad because he/they would stay the course with single-minded obsession.

So, Shanna would start stocking-up supplies, in case the antidote became necessary. Otto would happily repeat failed strategies just for the sake of the sheer destruction. Because, even assuming you avoided a maddened rampage, now you had a population of giant beasts with reptilian to avian-intelligence, some weighing a hundred-tons *before* being infected, that were now magnified by a factor of ten.

Shanna's strategy for dealing with these surviving giants was to give them room and get out of their way. They already had a natural tendency to spread out – their sense of territory was magnified with the rest of them.

There were also more direct methods Shanna used to goose them along. She got the big sauropods migrating south, using the rex-pack like sheep-dogs, chasing them towards the giant California redwoods – a nearer match for their food-requirements, especially after a few introduced nutrients into the local soil.

But that was still short-term. Until now, infected-giants never lived long enough to reproduce. Queenie would be the first.

Shanna didn't know what to expect. Theoretically, egg-laying giants shouldn't be able to reproduce easily. With proportionately-thicker shells, Shanna would have said it should be impossible.

But that was the nature of the Food of the Gods – it wasn't just some super-growth-hormone.

It really *was*, as her father put it, harnessing the chemical power of evolution – it didn't just *expand* an organism or else, geometrically, the animal would collapse. Rather, it *evolved* it – with size, came subtle changes in bone length and width, tendon thickness, and attachment points. The Food of the Gods left a very changed beast behind.

And while Shanna was in tune with *all* the new wildlife, her *shine* was stronger with the giants.

Maybe because the same thing that made the Food of the Gods possible was the purification element drawn from Shanna's own blood.

Like everything else in the new world, it came from her DNA first.

That was also why Shanna looked at it all as her responsibility.

And she was actually quite worried about what was happening offshore with Mark and Tom.

The military called it an *ocean-bloom,* when the infection spread undersea.

It was actually quite a grotesque scene. Once the first wave of infected giants died, their floating carcasses, mountains of leftover carrion, waited like poisoned bait.

The indigenous fauna went first. The Food of the Gods was always fatal, but with non-engineered organisms, it was disgustingly just-short of instantly, as ingestion of infected-carrion caused a breakdown at the cellular-level.

Local scavengers, even crustaceans and maggots, literally popped, their clouding blood attracting even more, causing mass dead-zones of natural wildlife.

The process *did*, eventually, break down the infected bio-matter, congealing it into kind of a sludgy-puss, floating at the surface like grease, until it broke up sufficiently to sink, blending into the sea-floor.

Shanna had tracked these areas of ocean that experienced blooms. While small amounts of the Food of the Gods was enough to infect an entire animal, she *believed* the minimal sheer bio-matter accumulated along the bottom should be safe.

These spots *did* tend to see a bit of odd flora. Perhaps it was not a true mutagen, but animals tended to grow large. There were also odd variances in color. And sometimes behavior.

And oddly, the local plant fauna thrived – and that might even be a *good* thing. Perhaps, after being filtered through enough destruction and death, the bio-waste of the Food of the Gods might actually achieve a measure of what it had been theoretically created for.

Of course, long-term effects in these areas still remained to be seen.

After KT-day, there was no going back to the nature that was before, although truthfully, there never was a true equilibrium – that was an illusion created by the constant progressive war between species, from insect to plant, fish to reptile, or mammal, a conflict with a ninety-nine-percent casualty rate. Reality was constant change, and the new wildlife had simply joined – or *re*-joined – the ecosystem, to be selected for survival or extinction all over again.

As were they all.

And extinction-events were triggered when things suddenly changed – like when an invasive species appeared. The encroachment of the Megalodons was significant.

Tom was right. It indicated Otto.

Shanna hadn't sensed the little bastard, but she *was* feeling edgy, as if premenstrual. Leanne was testy as well, although that was more easily tossed-off to hormones.

But if Otto was about, *something* was afoot, because it simply wasn't possible there wasn't.

Tom, who still liked to be called '*Major Tom*', was a good man to have on-site – a former astronaut, with a science background.

He had also told Shanna about being rescued from the Yucatan, and the death-ship he encountered there.

The site of the KT-asteroid.

Like Tom himself, Shanna wondered what Otto had in mind there. Her own island was sunk by popping just one volcano-cap. The KT-impact destroyed the world.

You had to expect the worst.

That was another reason they were lucky to have Tom there – he understood the little lizard well.

Since Tom first came to the Valley, Shanna had assigned him the informal position of Homeland Security, after they caught a small troop of Ottos trying to sneak a 'baby-nuke' into the Valley – a tactical warhead, lifted from some unknown site.

On that particular occasion, Big Red sniffed the little lizards out and simply stomped them flat – the warhead hadn't fired.

Hoping not to employ *that* method again, Shanna tasked Tom with hunting up any errant nukes that might still be out there.

Tom had already been cataloging potential nuclear threats. In the years after KT-day, the army rooted out most surviving assets across the continent. Otto, himself, had inadvertently gone a long way to destroying most nuke-sites overseas.

But there were still power plants, which meant labs, and access to equipment. Otto was not creative, but nuclear technology was known science. He could *make* a bomb.

Of course, there weren't as many Ottos as there used to be. Draco's mind-wipe had taken a large toll on the immediate region.

It was too bad, Shanna thought. Given time, the Dragon Lord might have been capable of wiping the little lizard out completely.

That might have been common ground.

Unfortunately, Draco's primary focus was *human*-extinction – he just wasn't a general nihilist. Draco wanted a pristine world to live in, without the pestilence of two-legged, hominid-rats.

Otto was about taking *everything* apart.

It had been less than a year since the fall of the Dragon Lord, and the scaly little bastard already attempted a nuclear attack on the Valley.

They didn't restrict themselves to nukes, either. Besides the odd rampage of rage-infected monsters, there were commando-raids from their sickle-claw minions, not to mention a whole range of conventional explosives, from military to industrial.

Once, they'd even introduced a super-virus, but Shanna's immune system fought it off, producing an antibody that spread just as fast.

But you never knew what was coming next. And these were just attacks against the Valley. Who knew what was going on everywhere else? The little bastard basically had the unchallenged run of the whole rest of the planet.

A *'quantum-gremlin'*, Tom called him. Shanna would agree – a gremlin that never stopped, or even truly slept.

So what came next?

"Maybe a Hiroshima Fat-Boy bomber-thing," Tom speculated after the baby-nuke incident, "and just get some bird or pterosaur to drop it. Or fly a plane himself, I guess." Tom shook his head. "It actually makes me wonder why he hasn't."

"Because he hasn't thought of it," Shanna replied. "His creative process is limited."

Although, if what she suspected about Otto's range of perception held true, there was her father's entire lifetime of nightmares to draw upon.

Who knew what was the next horror he might draw out of the id?

Shanna dearly hoped she hadn't sent Mark and

Tom to their deaths trying to find out.

When they radioed-in about the death-ship, she knew tailing it would be dangerous.

They both had wives – Mark's was pregnant.

But they also knew if Otto was there, they were probably already *in* extreme danger. And maybe the whole Valley, or the entire region itself.

It was going on two hours now, and still no word from them.

Outside, Big Red was posed in a cat-like pseudo-sleep, his eyes slitted, at rest, but alert – tense and aware.

Shanna decided to keep Lucas and the big red rex patrolling the borders today.

After all, it wasn't paranoia if they were really out to get you – and somewhere out there, they *were*.

CHAPTER 5

Lily and her daughter Sabrina stood on-deck of the death-ship. They had gained distance – the other boat was now out of sight.

One of the Ottos hopped up on Sabrina's shoulder and squawked.

In an instant, the pack of sickle-claws lined-up along the railing fell back, hooting like pirates, disappearing to their roosts below deck.

Sabrina patted the little lizard on her shoulder like a pet.

Lily scanned the empty ocean, looking for any sign of their tail. She saw nothing, but knew the other boat was still following them.

She also knew Mark was onboard – she could *feel* things like that now.

Sabrina, just eighteen, was beginning to as well. Something about that other boat had gotten her attention and Lily could see she didn't know why.

As far as Sabrina knew, her father was a man who died when the Mount fell – a soldier, named Stevens, who Lily had latched onto shortly after she arrived at the Mount, and who had no idea she was already pregnant.

Ironically, Sabrina knew her real father by name. When she had been a runaway from the Mount, it was none other than Mark, himself, having no idea who she was, who stumbled upon her, lost in the forest, and escorted her over the mountain.

The first time they'd met, he saved her life.

Mark was like that. Now that Lily thought about it, that was how *she* met him.

Unfortunately, neither instance ended well. Like mother, like daughter.

Lily had raised Sabrina on the Mount with a Coven of dragon-worshipers as aunts and mentors.

Now that the Mount had fallen – or more accurately, after she and her Coven sisters helped *destroy* it – the two of them were the last of the sisterhood left alive, and Lily was belatedly having second-thoughts.

Sabrina, who had never known anything else, was having difficulty with her mother's shift in attitude.

The Otto perched on Sabrina's shoulder chittered suspiciously, as if picking up on Lily's thought. This particular little creature was half-paralyzed and gimpish, as if from a debilitating stroke – a product of Draco's mind-wipe.

Without this one little lizard, Sabrina would have died in the wilderness, after she unknowingly fled her own father. The gimpy little beast led her to the Valley where she and Lily, who was arriving with the Mount's refugees, had found each other.

But the Valley, a virtual Shamballa for almost every other human survivor, was tyrannosaur-territory, and Otto simply couldn't be anywhere near. Instead, they continued north.

Their little lizard guide led them up into the hills surrounding the Puget Sound naval shipyard. It was long-since destroyed as a workable base, but enough supplies were left behind to last two people and a two-foot lizard.

They lived there seven months, set-up in a bayside condo, overlooking the water. It was actually kind of nice.

Then, a month ago, their gimpy Otto started talking, using phrases they hadn't heard before. The next morning, they woke to find a dozen more of the little lizards waiting on their front porch.

And a troop of sickle-claws. Lily knew her dromaeosaurs, and recognized leopard-sized *Deinonychus antirrhopus*. There were at least two-dozen – probably more in the brush. They postured around the courtyard like strutting roosters.

More imposingly, standing above *them,* were a pack of ten carcharodonts, all adult males, each over fifty-feet and nine-tons.

The Otto on Sabrina's shoulder chittered.

Before Lily realized what she intended, her daughter stepped forward and extended her hand to the nearest sickle-claw.

The creature's head darted quickly, as if to bite. Lily's heart skipped a beat.

But the creature just sniffed Sabrina's hand like a dog.

Then one of the big carcharodonts – it looked like Giganotosaurus – leaned in, its nostrils quivering.

The six-foot jaws parted.

Then the Ottos all squawked together and the big carnosaur stopped. With a low growl, it pulled back. Lily could see its throat flexing, reflexively swallowing.

Another moment, and it would have snapped Sabrina up like a dog taking a biscuit.

That was a month ago. Since then, Lily and Sabrina had been put to work in the naval-yard, loading up an old-world oil-rig, docked in the harbor, and simultaneously being salvaged and refurbished.

Lily didn't understand most of the equipment she was handling, but she and her daughter were useful for their thumbs.

Rather than end up like the other sisters, they did what they were told, but Lily was quite relieved when the boat was loaded, and appeared ready to set sail.

They had a lot of explosives onboard – demolitions-equipment, mostly.

Although Lily *did* recognize the nuclear atom-symbol on that last container she and Sabrina wheeled in.

It would not be Lily's first nuke – you saw that sort of thing when you ran with Otto and the sisterhood.

Both, Lily was deciding, were ultimately bad influences.

She had no idea what Otto's plans were this time – it wasn't like he asked her. She would cling to her blissful ignorance, and let them sail away and be gone.

But when Lily had taken her daughter's hand, turning for the dock, Sabrina's gimpy Otto hopped off her shoulder, screeching.

Sabrina looked at her mother.

"I think he wants us to go *with* them," she said.

"What for? Thumbs?" Lily shook her head. "No. I don't think so."

But when she turned, there were two sickle-claws blocking their path.

At the end of the dock, that big carcharodont eyed them hungrily.

The beasts were not growling – not yet – still playing nice.

But the message was clear. There were no choices here.

So, now, two days later, they found themselves miles out on the open ocean, the only two living humans on a death-ship.

When they first spotted that other ship on the horizon, Lily's first thought was actually about possible escape.

Then she felt that telltale touch.

According to Ginger and Luna, her senior sisters, Shanna's presence magnified *every* woman's natural empathic aura, but Lily was a bright light all on her own.

That was why she knew Mark was aboard that boat.

But she also knew a lot about him that had nothing to do with any empathic shine.

She knew, for example, that Mark had a wife and daughter in town. In point of fact, Lily had known Sally and Dawn for seventeen years at the Mount. During that time, Lily was the only person there who knew who Dawn's father really was, let alone that Mark was still alive.

Sabrina and Dawn would both be scandalized to learn they were sisters. Growing-up, they had *not* gotten along.

But Lily never told.

Secrets, however, were not easy to keep in the Valley. When Lily first arrived, she felt Shanna's presence shining on her like a prison spotlight.

Otto or no Otto, *that* was the real reason they fled north.

That and one other.

While they were still camped in the surrounding hills, Lily had taken a brief detour to the coast – the fishing community where Mark lived.

She couldn't let it go. She had come with a lifetime of training and morality learned from her sisters on the street.

It had been two weeks since Mark had taken his new family home.

Lily scoped-out his house from a grassy knoll, a quarter-mile up the hill. She had a hunting rifle purloined from town, and waited for Sally to come out.

She had not taken Sabrina along on this occasion – she didn't want her daughter to know.

It came down to seconds.

When Sally appeared however, Lily felt something new.

Another glow.

Sally, Lily realized, was a little bit knocked-up.

Sabrina's new half-sister.

Somehow, Lily knew it would be a sister.

With that sudden knowledge, cutting through the hateful, girlish jealousy, came a moment of clarity – a late, midlife bout of maturity.

Lily felt pangs of something she'd jettisoned long ago, after the first time she'd slid, underage, down a pole for some forty-something drunk – the sting of shame.

She dropped her rifle-sights from Sally's unsuspecting back, and fled.

Her intent was to let Mark and Sally live their lives. She would do her best to live hers.

Unfortunately, Otto had other plans.

The sisterhood treated the little lizard like a sage – the voice of the Dragon – and they had helped him nearly destroy the world.

If Lily's newfound maturity had afflicted her with a conscience, that was going to be a lot to live with.

It would *not*, however, stop her from doing what she was told.

While living in the relative safety of the Mount, she obeyed her Coven sisters, because they were her mentors, and because she *believed*.

Now, she did what she was told because she was afraid.

Funny how one thing led to another.

The Coven's dream – '*total matriarchal Amazon rule*', as Michelle phrased it – was something Lily could get behind, even if it meant offing a few old-guard patriarchs.

Extermination of her species was not what she signed-up for.

Otto had a nuke. Lily knew that couldn't bode well for the Valley. And after the Mount, there were damn few people left.

Although, in the short-term, if *she* was still there, if Sabrina was, they weren't extinct yet. Lily had to focus on their own immediate survival.

It was clear their on-going participation wasn't optional.

And lest her misgivings be for nothing, their last chore before their ship sailed, was to inject each of the carcharodonts with minute doses out of a small vial their gimpy little Otto kept for safekeeping – a souvenir from the Mount.

A vial that glowed plutonium-green.

Minute doses, so it didn't act *too* fast.

Half-a-dozen Ottos split from the rest, scrambling up onto the big carcharodonts' backs like birds riding a herd of elephants.

The largest of the carnosaurs, the one that had nearly eaten Sabrina, blinked with new alertness as its eyes already began to glow.

With Otto perched on its back, the big carcharodont turned, leading the procession away.

They were headed south, Lily presumed, towards the Valley.

The ship's destination remained uncertain. Over the past two days, their course was generally south, but mostly out to sea.

Mark's boat was the first thing they'd seen.

Lily shut her eyes – she could feel him out there.

She glanced at her fiery-eyed daughter and knew she could feel it too.

The Otto perched on Sabrina's shoulder chittered as if in disapproval.

Lily eyed the little lizard balefully, wondering again why she and her daughter had been forced to come.

She still had no idea where they were going, or *why* they needed a nuke out here in the middle of the ocean.

Sabrina patted the little lizard, unconcerned.

Lily knew that was her own fault – Sabrina had been taught to trust the snake.

To be fair, Lily was taught the same.

But now she was having her doubts.

Call it a crisis of faith.

CHAPTER 6

"Our orca friends are back," Pete called down from the boat-house.

Tom and Mark were both on deck with the crew, and before they even turned to the railing, the water beside them broke with twenty and thirty-foot, black-and-white Harlequinned bodies, breaching like dolphins.

As the pod paraded past, hovering near the front were three females – recognizable by their smaller, hooked dorsal fins, but clearly of different eco-types.

"This is at least three pods," Mark said. "Those females are probably the leaders. Orcas are a matriarchal culture. Big mama calls the shots."

Indeed, the rest of the sizable herd seemed to be hanging on these three females, who were now slapping the water with their tails and pectoral fins, in a clear play for attention.

"The big ones are transients," Mark identified. "They eat sea mammals like seals and whales. The little guys are the open-ocean shark-hunters."

Mark frowned, shaking his head.

"But that perky gal there," he said, indicating the twenty-foot female, who was now sky-hopping, as if looking for direct eye-contact. "She's a resident. You find them up in Puget Sound, or the bays and coves up into Canada. They eat salmon. They usually aren't this far out in open ocean.

"And," he added, "you *never* see these ecotypes interacting."

"How long since you've seen any orcas around here?" Tom asked.

"Not since before KT-day," Mark acknowledged. "They *are* very adaptive animals. I guess this might be the new normal."

The crew gathered to the railing, an audience for the performing orcas. Palmer and Wade, rough-trade to Tom's eye, were both wide-eyed as kids. Even the old veterans, Perry and Russell, watched, fascinated.

Jimmy looked back over his shoulder.

"What do you think they want?" he asked.

Tom shrugged to Mark. It seemed obvious enough.

"I think," he said, "they want us to follow."

"Why?" Mark asked dubiously.

"There must be something they want us to see," Tom replied.

He looked out at the circling fins, and wondered if this was about Otto.

Orcas weren't just smart, they were also empathic, sensitive, emotional creatures. It was not inconceivable that they responded negatively to the little lizard's presence.

"Maybe," Tom ventured, "they want to investigate too, but they want us to go first."

Mark sighed, resigned. He turned, climbing back up to the boathouse.

"I'll keep an eye on the sonar," he said.

Mark relieved Pete at the wheel, tapping his sonar screen and setting the range to maximum. It instantly started beeping, reporting the movements of the circling orcas.

"Anything else?" Tom asked, climbing up behind.

Mark shook his head.

"Not yet," he said. "But we just passed over a drop-off, and the water here is very deep."

Tom nodded soberly. They both knew what that meant.

Megs were like Great White sharks. They attacked from below, starting down deep. *This* was where they would hide.

Especially, if there were pliosaurs about.

Mark's sonar showed nothing definitive, but the depth-gauge indicated a drop of at least two-thousand feet. It was like they'd sailed over a massive volcanic vent, descending deep into the earth.

"Can you pan back?" Tom asked. "Just get general geography?"

Mark shrugged, and tapped the screen. The sonar pings stopped and the underwater map pulled back.

According to the screen, they were at the edge of a large semi-circular drop-off – the curve of the underwater canyon ran for miles in each direction.

Tom blinked as he realized what they were looking at.

This was something else in common with what he'd seen in the Gulf.

It was a crater-site.

There had always been speculation that the cataclysm that killed the dinosaurs was brought about by more than one asteroid. Tom knew they had found several other concurrent impact-craters than just the Yucatan Chicxulub-site.

Was this another one?

Tom didn't know if KT-day circa sixty-five-million B.C. was the result of several asteroids in succession, or one larger original breaking apart as it approached the system – the simple rotation of the Earth could account for the disparity of the locations among the known sites. It would have also maximized the ecological damage if several asteroids struck within days, or even hours.

Conventional theory maintained that a single impact did most of the damage. The Yucatan-site was always the most likely culprit.

But the crater Tom was looking at now was a *lot* larger than Chicxulub.

"Hey guys," Pete said behind them. "Look at this."

Pete had a pair of binoculars and found something on the horizon.

'What have you got?" Mark asked.

Pete handed over the glasses. Mark focused-in on what looked like a deep-sea oil-drilling-platform. He handed the scopes to Tom, who nodded.

"I think it's time to check in with Shanna," he said.

CHAPTER 7

Kristie was waiting at Shanna's house when Tom and Mark finally radioed in.

Shanna had also contacted Sally, who lived on the coast, seventy-miles west, in the fishing community that had grown adjacent to the Valley. Communication was mostly done with old-style radio and CBs, and Shanna had raised Sally an hour ago.

She sent both their husbands after a death-ship – they deserved to hear it from her.

Kristie, who knew Tom would have gone anyway, joined Shanna at her house, pacing by the radio.

Sally, who knew Mark wouldn't, simply asked to keep tabs.

Shanna knew Sally was late in her third trimester.

"Dawn's with me," Sally assured her, as if reading Shanna's thoughts.

"I'll keep in touch," Shanna promised.

She wished she could offer more than that, but Tom's report wasn't good. With Otto involved, that was not a light statement.

An underwater crater. And a drilling rig.

"Compared to Chicxulub, I'd say it's easily twice the size," Tom estimated.

Shanna knew there was no quick way to date it, but based on their mapped location, it was half-a-day's rotation of the Earth from the Yucatan-site, north and west.

Kristie's concerns were more immediate.

"You've seen Megs?" she asked.

"We've seen a few," Tom acknowledged. "And more on sonar. One of them was chased off by that pod of orcas. They went right after it. Just kind of beat it up."

Shanna's brows raised. *That* was something she wouldn't have expected.

"And they led you there?"

"Just like Lassie," Tom replied. "They wanted us to see this."

"How close are you to the drilling-rig? Is it in operation?"

"We're a ways out, yet," Tom said. "You want us to check it out?"

Shanna would very much like to know what was happening on that rig, but she guessed the on-staff personnel would be inhospitable.

Mark would have weapons onboard, but he wasn't outfitted to take on a battalion of sickle-claws.

They had planes and choppers in the Valley, Shanna decided. Mark and Tom could mark the location, and then she could send Cameron and Maverick with a crew that *was* sufficiently armed.

Best not to tarry much further. Shanna nodded to Kristie.

"I'm going to call them back," she said.

But then a sudden beep sounded over the radio.

"Whoops," Mark said in the background. "I just got a *big* hit on sonar."

"How big?" Shanna asked quickly. "What have you got?"

"Uhhh," Mark replied, unhappily, "*big.*"

They could hear the beeping sonar.

"*Blooming* big, if you take my meaning," Mark said.

Shanna shut her eyes.

"It's a Meg," Mark said. "It's still a mile or so out, but it's closing."

Kristie eyed Shanna grimly. Mark's boat was the biggest and sturdiest in the fleet, but that didn't matter with an infected giant.

"Turn around," Shanna said. "Get out of there now."

There was a momentary pause and they heard Mark barking instructions in the background, accompanied by increasingly loud sonar beeps.

"What's happening?" Shanna asked, trying not to sound helpless, but the scene was already playing out behind her eyes.

"Well," Mark said, "we are going to run like hell. Unfortunately, the time to have done that was an hour ago. If that Meg is targeting us, we aren't going to outrun it."

Shanna shut her eyes. They had choppers in the Valley – Maverick could be in the air in twenty minutes, but they were *miles* out into the open ocean. Whatever was going to happen would be over and done.

Nevertheless, she tapped the radio.

"Mark? Tom? I'm sending Maverick with a chopper out after you."

Kristie met her eye thankfully.

They waited a moment, but there was no response.

"Mark?" Shanna said. "Tom?"

Dead silence.

Kristie looked up at Shanna, her face going pale.

For a heartbeat, Shanna was torn – she was about to call Maverick. But before she could switch channels, both Cameron and Maverick burst in the front door.

"*Honey?*" Cameron called urgently, panting as if he'd been running. "We've got problems."

Maverick was holding his own radio.

"I just got off the horn with Lucas," he said. "He and Big Red are at the northern border. They've got carcharodonts.

"*Blooming* carcharodonts," he added.

Shanna blinked. She had literally felt nothing – no presence at all. Was Otto already back in sufficient numbers to hide from her so completely?

"At least ten infected giants," Cameron said. "Lucas has Big Red and the rex-pack already on the way."

Otto, Shanna thought grimly. Whatever malfeasance he was up to, this was part of it.

The rest had something to do with an asteroid impact-point that once ended the world.

From the north crest of the Valley, she heard the first rumbles of false thunder.

Shanna looked out her window. Up on the hill, she saw the giant, dragon-like monoliths, standing high above the trees.

She could see the green glow in their eyes.

Like a breaking storm, their bellowing roars echoed off the mountains.

Waiting in the Valley below, Big Red and the pack of *T. rex* responded in kind.

CHAPTER 8

The Meg that hit them was over six-hundred feet – the trawler was like a seal in the jaws of a Great White.

Mark didn't see it coming until the last moment. He was focused on the shark chasing them, but this attack came from below – a second Meg.

The sonar beeped the warning. They were already targeted – there was no chance.

Mark's eyes cut grimly to Tom as he hit the switch on the loudspeaker, broadcasting his voice across the deck.

"Abandon ship!"

Mark and Tom both broke for the deck. The crew was trying to dislodge the lifeboats, but it was already too late.

"Jump!" Mark shouted, and obeying himself, he ran for the railing, grabbing Jimmy as he went, shoving the Jonas brothers ahead of him, and leaped overboard.

Tom was half-a-step behind, followed by Lumpy, Russell, and then Perry, Wade, and Palmer, in running succession, just as the Meg struck from below.

It was actually the sheer force of the attack that saved them – the displaced water under the boat surged and the men were thrown clear, avoiding the direct impact of a six-hundred-foot shark hitting their boat hard enough to clear the water by its full-body length.

Tom felt himself tumbling, first through water and then into the air, as he was sent spinning. He flew nearly a hundred-yards before hitting the cement-hard water.

He struggled, dazed, splashing to the surface – and looked up just in time to see the Meg poised in mid-leap, a bare moment before it came crashing back down, the trawler still latched in its jaws – it hovered like a giant oak, about to tumble, not yet sure which way to fall.

Tom watched helpless, waiting to be crushed like a bug, but the Meg fell back the other way.

It was a *very* brief reprieve – when the giant shark hit the water, it sent cascading tidal waves in every direction.

Tom was pretty sure he drowned somewhere in the middle, as he was tossed like limp flotsam.

He was semi-conscious, struggling weakly ten-feet under the surface, and was pretty close to his last few seconds on Earth, when a large black shape rose up from below.

Instinctive fear jerked his exhausted limbs spasmodically, but the shape came up too quickly, and Tom was suddenly being pushed to the surface.

When his head broke water, he found himself hanging onto the black dorsal fin of an orca.

It was one of the senior females, the resident-pod's matriarch. She was carrying him away from the wreck.

Once his tearing eyes cleared enough to look around, he saw the other two matriarchs on either side. Mark clung to the fin of the larger, transient female, and Pete rode cowboy-style across the back of the shark-hunter.

Tom also saw Jimmy and Big Jonas clinging to orca fins – Lumpy was there. Tom couldn't see any others.

A headcount would have to wait.

He looked back after the wreck. The Meg that hit them had disappeared, but Tom was sure it hadn't gone far. The first shark also sounded, no doubt going deep, scouting targets on the surface.

The orca pod clustered close around the matriarchs. Tom hoped they were keeping a good watch below. Orcas had sonar, but these sharks were infected-giants. Once they got a head of steam, those battleship-sized jaws were hard to avoid.

Mark waved to Tom, as he clung like a jockey to the resident-matriarch's back.

"Where are they taking us?" he hollered over.

Tom actually hadn't thought to wonder about that yet. But now that he looked ahead, their destination was clear.

They were making a beeline for the drilling-rig.

CHAPTER 9

Tom went to an aquatic park once as a kid, where trainers rode captive orcas. They made it look like they were gliding effortlessly through the water.

In reality, it felt like being dragged through the waves by a five-ton truck. The resident-matriarch porpoised along at thirty-knots, although she was, at least, mindful of her passenger, keeping near the surface.

As they approached the drilling-rig, Tom looked back for the Megs.

He spotted one of the fins, cruising like a sixty-foot sailboat, hovering the perimeter like a sentry. But the shark did not approach the rig.

The resident-matriarch circled over to where a small dock was stationed for smaller boats, with a ladder built up the support strut to the main deck.

Tom felt his stomach drop, as the big female abruptly reared and washed him up onto the platform with a wave, ducking back below the surface with barely a ripple.

A moment later, Mark was lofted up beside him, followed by Big Jonas, Jimmy and Pete.

Tom counted five others – Lumpy the cook, Palmer and Wade, Perry, and Russell.

Only one lost. As Big Jonas climbed up onto the dock, he looked back at the ocean after his missing little brother.

Out on the water, the orcas also disappeared.

Once they made their drops, the matriarchs sounded. The rest of the pod followed in an instant, and the clustered jetty of black fins vanished beneath the surface.

Both Megs remained circling. But there were probably more – likely infected-giants.

Tom had no doubt they could take out this platform without much more trouble than their boat, especially several of them.

But the Megs hovered at distance, circling steadily.

Tom and Mark looked up the ladder leading up to the main platform.

Mark nodded – *after you.* Tom grabbed the first rung and began to climb. Mark followed with the rest.

Whatever was waiting up above, they were walking into it unarmed except for a few pocket-knives.

Tom actually had a brief pause for hope when he reached the top and looked out onto an empty platform.

"It looks clear," he called back.

The others clambered up in procession on-deck beside him.

And it *looked* clear until they walked into the open.

Then, a troop of leopard-sized sickle-claws leaped down from their guard perches atop the platform's roof. More came running from the side-deck.

Tom had already scouted out the main bridge and now he simply bolted for the tower.

"Run!" he shouted.

Mark launched into a sprint beside him, and the

crew made a break across the deck.

Tom slammed bodily into the door, wrenching it open, even as he heard the first human scream. Palmer was a big fellow, not much of a runner, and the sickle-claws ran him right down.

Perry was next. There was a ripping sound as the old fisherman was gutted, still standing. Perry gasped, trying to scream as the clawed devils bore him to the ground.

"Come on!" Tom shouted, standing at the door, waving the others through. Pete and Mark pushed by together, with Jimmy and Big Jonas right behind. Lumpy and Wade piled through next – *last*, because Russell was taken down just a few steps short.

Tom was splattered with blood as he yanked the door shut. There was heavy impact as the dromaeosaurs struck a moment later, shaking the steel door on its frame.

In the closed space, the stench was foul – there was just enough light to see the old, crypt-gnawed bones of the former crew scattered randomly about.

The hallways were lined with cobwebs, like a spider-woven tunnel, descending into the dark – not from *human* passage – even a large dromaeosaur wasn't much more than four-feet at the hip.

But they sure looked big as hell when another troop of the clawed-devils came charging up the spider-passages out of the dark.

Tom was searching for the stairway to the operations office when he heard Mark blurt out behind him, "*Watch it!*"

Wade grunted as the first of the clawed-devils

pushed through the narrow hatchway and leaped upon him bodily, slashing with both seven-inch claws at once, and bicycling kicks once he was down. Wade was split open, spilling his entrails onto the floor.

That was how sickle-claws killed you.

It would have been all over, except their attackers were forced to crowd down the narrow hall.

Big Jonas and Lumpy, who once stalemated an arm-wrestling match for an hour, both grabbed boat-hooks off the wall. Big Jonas clubbed the creature posed over Wade across the back of its neck like a fish.

There was a baseball crack of breaking bone, and the beast dropped. Big Jonas gave it a second smack for good measure. He turned to the others.

"Go!" he ordered.

Then he and Lumpy went in swinging as the sickle-claws came at them.

Tom made a break for the stairs. Mark pounded up behind him with Jimmy and Pete on his heels.

They heard Big Jonas cry out, outraged, in pain. *"Bastards!"*

Then his voice was cut off.

Lumpy went a moment later. There was a grunt and then fabric tearing-sounds.

Tom heard clawed feet on the stairs.

The rig's command office was mounted on the top deck like the boathouse on a ship. The door was standing ajar, and as he came running up, Tom pushed it open.

Otto was sitting at the desk – and the console – and the computer screen.

The little lizards jumped up, hissing, as the four

men suddenly piled through their door.

At the stairway behind them, the dromaeosaur pack had made the landing and were now charging down the hall.

Tom pulled the door shut – the heavy metal shook as the panther-sized beasts slammed into it broadside, careless of injury.

All three Ottos also leaped, their own miniature scythe-claws flailing.

Mark and Pete already had their knives drawn – a lifetime of slicing fish came in handy as they cut each of the leaping lizards in half at a stroke.

The third one caught its sickle in Pete's shirt, taking some skin underneath, before it fell away, twitching. Jimmy stepped forward and stomped on the half with the foot claws.

There was another heavy impact and the steel door-jamb shook.

Tom turned to Jimmy and Pete.

"Watch the door," he said.

The two looked doubtful, but stood ready, eyes fixed on the shaking frame.

Tom sat down at the console and tapped-up the computer screen, opening the workstation.

"Well," he said. "There it is. That's what they were working on."

He pointed to the red areas highlighted on the oceanographic map.

"This whole area of ocean is right above the crater," Tom said. "These are fissure points. We are right above a cluster of them. That's where they're drilling."

"Why?" Mark asked. "What do they want down there?"

"My guess?" Tom replied. "They've got

themselves a geological trigger-point. One that once caused a major extinction-event. I think he's trying to disrupt it or set it off somehow."

Tom nodded, regarding the blinking map.

"He's trying to trigger a seismic-event. He's done it in the past, with the San Andreas fault. He spent at least a year triggering eruptions across a thousand-miles of Rocky Mountains. And now he's drilling into a KT-impact-point."

"What in *God's* name could he have in mind this time?"

"I think he probably means to drop a nuke down that hole," Tom replied. "Last time, he split the continent. For all I know, he's trying to crack the whole damned planet in two."

Mark stared at him dumbfounded.

"Is he crazy?"

Tom said nothing. He once asked Shanna the same thing.

"He's a rational man's nightmares," she had replied. "I think they were my father's."

There was another tremendous impact at the door.

"Ummm," Pete said, doubtfully. "Does this place have a radio?"

Mark nodded, sliding his chair to the neighboring station, which was adorned with headphones, a microphone, and speakers. He switched the system on.

"I'm sending a distress beacon to Shanna. But we're in a lot more immediate trouble than that." He tossed a thumb at the shaking door. "That's not going to hold."

Tom looked back at the steel door, which was probably capable of resisting a sledge. But Pete and Jimmy were looking nervous as it rattled on its hinges.

Then the radio beeped for attention – a hailing frequency coming in.

There was the whine of static before a woman's voice sounded over the speakers.

"... hear me? Mark? I know you're there. Please answer."

The voice was not Shanna's.

Mark was shaking his head.

"It... *couldn't* be..."

Behind them, Pete groaned.

"Hey guys?" Jimmy said, moving to the window. "We've got company."

Tom knew what it was before he even turned to look.

Outside, the death-ship had reappeared, escorted by a procession of giant, infected Megs.

It was pulling up to dock.

CHAPTER 10

The ship docked normally, no different than it would have twenty years ago, before the world ended.

Watching it happen now was like seeing a ghost-car drive itself. Or a brontosaurus skeleton walk bare-bones down the street.

"Mark?" the woman said again over the radio. "Are you there? It's me, Lily."

Then, more definitely.

"I *know* you're there. Please. Just come out on deck."

The radio signal clicked off.

Across the way, two slight figures appeared on the top deck of the death-ship. Tom recognized both Lily and her daughter, Sabrina, from the Mount.

He glanced sideways at Mark and remembered they were mutual acquaintances.

Mark stepped out onto the railed deck just outside the tower-office. Tom followed.

The two women stood at the opposite railing. Packs of sickle-claws lined the roof and lower decks all around them.

There was a single Otto perched on Sabrina's shoulder.

Lily waved over shyly.

"It's been a long time, Lily," Mark called over. "Up to dickens, again?"

"Mark..." Her voice broke briefly. "I didn't

want to be here."

"Seems I've heard things like that before," Mark replied.

The Otto on Sabrina's shoulder chittered.

There was a loud, mechanical groan from below as a crane started-up, moving to pick up the crate being brought out on the deck of the death-ship.

Tom had a pretty good idea what that shipment was.

"Hey there, Lily? Sabrina? This is Major Tom. Remember me?"

Sabrina and Lily exchanged wide-eyes.

"Major Tom from the Mount?"

"Yep. And as I recall, you and your friends had a hand in bringing it down."

He waved at the crane loading their cargo onto the rig, where it was immediately surrounded by sickle-claws and yammering Ottos.

"I don't suppose," Tom called over, "that you happened to have brought a nuke with you? Like the one that nearly got detonated in the Valley a few months ago?"

Lily said nothing – answer enough.

Behind them, there was a fusillade of blows at the steel door.

"Guys?" Pete said nervously. "I don't think we've got much time."

Tom didn't think so either.

"I don't want to see you get hurt," Lily called over.

"You seem to go back-and-forth on that," Mark returned.

But now he tipped his head to Sabrina.

"So... am I to understand this is your daughter?"

Lily hesitated, glancing at Sabrina, who blinked

back, uncertainly. Lily nodded.

"She tells me," Lily said, "that you've met."

Mark fell silent.

Tom nodded as understanding dawned – he could now guess what Mark's past must have been with Lily.

Sabrina had Mark's eyes.

Mark crooked his head – a mannerism mimicked by Sabrina, as they both computed what now seemed obvious.

There was a heartbeat of silence as everyone knew each other.

The Otto on Sabrina's shoulder hissed.

On cue, there was another tremendous impact against the metal door. Pete and Jimmy looked back worriedly.

"The hinges are starting to go," Pete said.

Tom could hear the scrape of metal. Those dromaeosaurs were coming through.

Lily watched helplessly across the small divide. Sabrina was still staring wide-eyed at Mark.

But it was the death-ship itself that became a target first, as a giant pair of crocodile-jaws rose up from below, opening on either side.

Lily and Sabrina both screamed as the teeth smashed together, crushing the three-hundred-foot, twenty-thousand-pound tanker like a tin-can, splitting the hull across the middle.

The bloom had obviously infected local pliosaurs too.

And just like *T. rex*, they *hated* Otto.

The lizard on Sabrina's shoulder squawked – both she and Lily were sent flying as the boat itself was knocked into the air – which was lucky because the giant pliosaur turned and yanked the crushed death-ship under the surface like a crocodile taking an antelope.

Most of the sickle-claws were also pitched into the ocean, although Tom saw others jumping ship, leaping literally right out of the giant pliosaur's jaws.

Lily and Sabrina landed like rag-dolls in the water right below the drilling-rig's main tower. Tom saw them hit with a splash, and then both float limp.

Mark looked over the side – it was seventy-feet to the water. He glanced at Tom, then back at Pete and Jimmy.

The door behind them was going.

Mark climbed over the railing and stepped off, dropping into the ocean.

Tom looked back at the shaking door.

"Oh, what the hell."

He jumped after Mark, followed by Jimmy and Pete, just as the door finally broke open and the marauding sickle-claws pushed their way in.

Tom's stomach fluttered as he fell, and then he felt the icy-sting and jarring impact, as he hit the water.

He came up sputtering, and was instantly aware of several sickle-claws swimming in the water beside him. But for the moment, at least, they seemed mostly concerned with simply staying afloat.

"Tom!" Mark's voice shouted over the waves.

The swells underneath the platform rose high enough for Tom to see Mark. He had Lily's unconscious form in a lifeguard's pose.

"Where's Sabrina?" Mark shouted.

"I've got her," Pete hollered over.

He and Jimmy were pulling themselves up on one of the oil-rig's floating struts underneath the main platform. They had Sabrina, who appeared groggy but conscious. She was struggling in their grip, even as they pulled her out of the water.

There was a chitter as that gimpy Otto that had been sitting on her shoulder hopped up beside them.

"Oh, *Hell* no," Jimmy blurted and kicked the little lizard in a soccer-style punt. The little creature squawked, as it spun, limp and broken, back out into the water, and washed away.

"You *bastard!*" Sabrina screamed, suddenly fighting Pete's hands. Jimmy started to reach for her but she slapped him away.

"Get your hands *off* me!"

"*Jesus*," Jimmy returned, stepping back. "*Sorry.*"

His breath huffed out a moment later when he was cleaved from behind by a seven-inch scythe-hook, as the first of the swimming dromaeosaurs scrambled up out of the water, and split him open down the back.

Jimmy gagged and kicked as the jaguar-sized beast bore him down.

Pete had his knife out in a flash, lashing out across the dromaeosaur's thin neck, cutting its throat. It kicked twice before it toppled back into the water, pulling Jimmy, who was not *quite* yet a corpse, entangled in its claws, along with it. They both disappeared with a splash.

Tom was half a length behind Mark, swimming for the platform, but now some of the other swimming sickle-claws turned in their direction.

With Lily on his shoulder, Mark reached up.

Pete took his hand, and was immediately joined by Sabrina, grabbing for her mother – together, they pulled them both onto the platform.

Tom swam for all he was worth, nearly careening face-first into the rigging as he lurched out of the water. Pete caught his hand and hauled him up.

The pursuing dromaeosaurs were close behind. They were strong swimmers, and would be on them in seconds. Pete had his knife out and ready.

But then, in the ocean just beyond, that giant pliosaur surfaced again, the death-ship still in its jaws, shaking the demolished boat in a crocodile-like death-roll.

Sitting there at the surface, it was hit by two Megs at once.

The pliosaur was knocked completely clear of the water as both sharks, six-hundred-feet each, struck from below in simultaneous Polaris-attacks. The giant reptile was bitten in half and quartered. The two Megs crashed together in mid-air before tumbling back to the water with a tidal splash.

"Oh, *shit*," Tom blurted, as he saw the wave coming, "*Hang on!*"

Mark grabbed Lily, and Pete grabbed Sabrina, as the water flooded past.

The sickle-claws were washed past the platform with it.

When the swell settled, Tom saw the two circling Megs, their sixty-foot fins patrolling the perimeter.

But Tom also saw the humpback shapes of several more pliosaurs, as well, moving in a gang – all infected-giants – closing in.

Tom looked up at the platform, doubtfully.

Above were packs of sickle-claws.

Not that the platform looked to survive long anyway.

The circling Megs had been joined by others. Tom counted at least six, and probably more circling below.

And now the pliosaurs were moving in.

CHAPTER 11

Shanna had not expected such a direct ground-assault on the Valley itself – Otto had sent infected giants their way before, but never a deliberate attack-squad of giant carcharodonts.

Leanne and Kristie huddled beside her and together they watched the confrontation on the hillside unfold. Leanne was already smarting at being held in the rear – a product of her *condition*. And right now her husband was sitting on the back of a two-hundred-foot *T. rex*, leading it into battle against even larger killers.

Now Shanna also heard the buzz of rotor-blades, indicating her own husband arriving on the front, as always, riding shotgun for Maverick, as they led their small air-force – in this case, four small search-and-rescue choppers Maverick's father had been restoring, flown by Maverick and three new recent recruits from the Mount.

Below, Lucas sat astride Big Red as the alpha rex led the pack, including the soon-to-be-expecting Queenie. A rex-female in her 'condition' was meaner than ever.

The pack was also joined by the Valley's delinquent males, Junior and Rudy, who both generally avoided Big Red's territory, along with a younger adolescent, Bucky, who just recently aged-out of the female pack.

Mature male tyrannosaurs tended to run by themselves, but they would make an exception for

Otto, particularly if there was an opportunity to kill carcharodonts – as alpha super-predators went, these big carnosaurs were the tyrannosaur's only true rivals. That was a conflict Shanna had seen play out many times.

Carcharodonts were always dangerous, but Otto seemed to guide them via their own reptilian-brain, activating instinctive impulses – attack, retreat, and defend. And they responded not at all to Shanna's own presence.

But Shanna or no Shanna, *T. rex* and carcharodonts were deadly enemies who would attack each other on sight.

That was usually the carcharodont's mistake, because direct assault on a rex put it face-first into the tyrannosaur's most powerful weapon – giant steel-trap jaws that had simply out-evolved the older, carnosaur-model.

On the other hand, the jaws of *Giganotosaurus carolinii* were specifically designed to take down the biggest sauropods in history, and could certainly kill a rex with an unguarded bite.

But that required judicious use of their tools – ordinarily not a carnosaur's strong suit, but was now provided by the little lizards perched like birds across their massive backs.

And *oh*, but their very *presence* egged-on the *T. rex* – they *hated* those little bastards. Shanna herself tasted that sting of psychic sulfur every time the scaly little rats were about. Leanne was wiping her eyes – she felt it too.

Up on the hill, the rex-pack was spoiling for the fight.

That was the disadvantage for the *T. rex* as they rose to defend the Valley.

Usually, tyrannosaurs had the mental edge over carcharodonts – larger-brained, strategy-oriented, ambush-style attackers. Today, the *T. rex* were emotional and half-cocked, which was never an advantage in a fight.

And today, the carcharodonts had jockeys.

The difference was evident as the battle was joined.

There were no formalities, when the rex pack got close enough, they charged.

Bucky was the first – pumping full of teenage testosterone, he could barely hold himself back on a normal day, let alone with Otto's scent in the air. The young male attacked, heedless of the carcharodonts' demonstrable size advantage, lunging forward, jaws agape.

But instead of engaging, the carnosaurs faded back, splitting to each side, treating Bucky like a charging sauropod.

You didn't physically engage sauropods – you got out of their way.

Then you bit them on the ass from behind.

It was simply initiating a different instinctive response, but it worked well on Bucky, who over-extended his strike, leaving him open as two carcharodonts lunged in from each side, and their saw-blade jaws slashed him open.

The first bite caught the young tyrannosaur across the ribs and belly, cleaving away a fold of flesh like a scythe. Bucky staggered as the wound promptly began spouting out his life-blood.

But the second bite caught his throat. The thick bulldog neck kept his head from being severed, but Bucky's jugular was slashed. The teenage rex stumbled and fell, already bleeding out.

There were not, Shanna thought grimly, many creatures that could do that to a rex.

Lizzie was next, half a step behind Bucky. She managed to get her teeth into one of her opponents – first blood for the home-team, but only a glancing strike, catching one of the retreating carnosaurs in the thigh, chopping out a chunk of meat, but the carcharodont jerked away, bellowing.

The carnosaur's fellows, however, hit Lizzie from behind, attacking the legs this time, hamstringing her. The big female howled, even as she dropped to the ground, crippled as a horse. The carcharodont she'd bit turned, angry and bleeding, and tore out her throat.

From Big Red's back, Lucas could see what was happening, and tried to yell a warning, but in Otto's presence, he was whistling in the wind.

Big Red did the first real damage, hitting the carcharodont bent over Lizzie's corpse. The big carnosaur turned to meet him but this time it was jaw-to-jaw, and Big Red had his weight behind a running charge – a Polaris-style attack on land. The carcharodont took the strike dead in the face and was killed on impact.

Queenie took out carcharodont number two as a second beast went after Big Red's unguarded flank. She caught the carnosaur's neck, wrenching it like a bull, breaking its spine, even as her teeth sank in, cleaving away most of his head.

But then she was hit by a third beast, attacking at her own back, slicing her deep along the hips and tail.

Fortunately, Queenie reflexively turned from the strike and only received a glancing slash, painful, but non-crippling. Outraged, she swung her massive head around, catching the carnosaur in the jaw like a sledge – the beast staggered.

Then it was hit by Junior and Rudy, followed immediately by Black Beauty and Tink – the unfortunate carcharodont was torn apart from four different directions.

The fight was deteriorating into a saloon brawl that favored the pit-bull tyrannosaurs, but then Shanna again felt that familiar sting in her senses.

Out on the battlefield, the carcharodonts abruptly postured, backing-off once again into the stalking/hunting mode, not letting the battle turn into a dogfight.

Then a shot rang out from Maverick's chopper. Cameron had scoped-out one of the Ottos and picked it off the giant carcharodont's back like a duck in a shooting gallery.

Maverick's voice sounded over the open radio.

"Shoot the lizards! What do I always tell ya? Shoot the goddamn lizards first."

In a moment, a barrage of shots sounded from the circling choppers, targeting the Ottos perched on the carnosaurs' backs. Shanna saw three Ottos chopped away in quick succession.

One of the carcharodonts lunged for the choppers, but this proved counterproductive as it left itself open – exploited almost immediately by Junior and Rudy, as they both hit the big carnosaur together, Rudy on the neck, Junior tearing open its gut.

The Ottos on the big carnosaur's back bolted as their mount fell, but were crushed as the dying giant hit the ground and rolled.

Shanna could feel the physic pressure in her head ease as each of the little lizards was taken out.

Correspondingly, the savvy tactical approach of the carnosaurs went with them.

Giganotosaurus, Shanna thought, was a rather dumb, particularly brutal beast, with a social-hierarchy like that of a primitive crocodile – they were aggressive and dominant with rivals.

In their day, these big carcharodonts were the thesis-statement super-predator nature ever evolved. Faced with the usurper, *T. rex*, they had but one response – they attacked with gaping jaws that were the deadliest their world had ever seen.

By *T. rex* standards, however, they were twenty-million-years obsolete. The rex-pack met them in the middle.

"Okay," Maverick said over the radio, "back off, fellas. I think Lucas' team can handle it from here."

The choppers pulled away as the giant warring theropods crashed together, locking jaws like pit-dog-fights, and began to tear away at each other – and that was where it quickly went south for the carcharodonts.

Big Red engaged the largest of them, and the giant carnosaur actually managed to latch onto his upper jaw, an advantage position that was completely nullified as the tyrannosaur simply bit down on its lower jaw, breaking it, and then chomping it away. The carcharodont staggered, falling to the tarmac as Big Red kicked it aside, charging immediately after the next.

Queenie's growls rose above the rest as she dragged her own opponent to the ground, breaking its neck, but continuing to shake it brutally, no doubt still aware of the bleeding slash across her own flank.

Black Beauty and Tink were also slashed and bleeding, but likewise bore their rivals down. Junior and Rudy worked in tandem, going for the carnosaurs' legs as the pack of them fell into disarray.

There was one big carcharodont, however, who held back, seemingly grown wise – or more likely, it was the three Ottos still perched on his back.

The beast circled, looking for Big Red's back, as the lead-rex focused its attention on the last of its fellows.

But Big Red had a jockey too. Lucas cried out a warning and the big red rex turned in time to intercept the assault, catching the carcharodont jaw-to-jaw, sinking his teeth deep, and biting the carnosaur's skull cleanly in half. Its dead body fell away, crashing to the earth, shaking the ground like a quake.

The Ottos on its back turned and ran for the brush.

And now that it looked to be over, the other remaining Ottos jumped ship as well, abandoning their charges as the rex-pack took the last of the carnosaurs down. The little lizards ran for the brush but the rex-pack was thorough, rooting out each one, stomping them flat, not stopping until the last straggler was accounted for.

Shanna felt their psychic-stench fade. It was not gone completely – they were still about, but not in the Valley.

Because *this*, she thought, looking out on the battlefield, as the rex-pack, now began to eat the carcasses of their carnosaur rivals, *this* didn't make any sense.

It was a deliberate coordinated attack. But it had not been an attempt to amass overwhelming forces like when the Mount had been taken down. This was a commando-squad.

Possibly a suicide mission – one with no obvious purpose.

That meant it was a distraction.

She turned her head west. Otto was still about. But their real presence was somewhere distant – like out at sea.

"Maverick?" Shanna said into the radio, "how's our perimeter looking? We haven't got any other surprises, do we?"

"I got a chopper circling the hills," Maverick sent back. "Nothing. Those big guys are hard to miss. Any little guys, the rex' nose should sniff 'em out."

Shanna nodded. Not the Valley then.

She turned to Kristie.

"I think," Shanna said, "we better go get your husband."

CHAPTER 12

The oil rig shook at its foundations – unlike the Megs, the giant pliosaurs had no qualms about destroying it. The hapless land-dwelling hominids clung to the structure's underbelly as the battle waged precariously close.

Tom could see something was wrong. He'd witnessed pliosaurs and Megs battle before, even infected-giants, but this was different.

In the Gulf, the Megs behaved like fish. Here today, they were implementing strategy.

"They're holding a deliberate perimeter around the rig," Tom said. "They're protecting it."

Mark glanced up to the rig above.

"Buying time enough to drop that nuke?"

Tom nodded soberly.

From the looks of things, this was an advanced stage of the operation. The hole into the crust of the crater was already dug – presumably, all that remained was to simply drop the bomb down the pipe. Tom wondered what kind of kilotonage they were playing with.

Mark looked at him unhappily.

"You wanna try and sabotage their drop, don't you?"

"Well," Tom said, "we could hang out here, and hope to survive another ten or twenty minutes while he instigates a global extinction-event."

Mark grumbled.

"I didn't want to come out here in the first

place."

But he stood, looking for an access ladder. He pulled Lily to her feet. She was still dazed.

"What's happening?"

"Well," Mark said, turning an arch eye to both her and Sabrina, "it seems your lizard-masters are about to drop a nuke down a fissure into a KT-impact-point. And we're about to get a good look at it."

Lily and Sabrina exchanged glances.

"*Why?*" Lily asked.

Tom hiccupped a bitter laugh.

"Because that's what he *does,*" he said. "There's literally nothing else *to* him. He breaks things. On a big scale. That's what he does. That's *all* he does."

He regarded Lily and Sabrina helplessly.

"You live on the planet too, right?"

Mark turned to the maintenance ladder.

"Not that the planet will matter much to *us* in the next few minutes anyway. You can come with us or not."

He started to climb. Tom followed. Lily exchanged doubtful looks with Sabrina, before moving to follow. Pete extended a helpful hand to Sabrina, but she slapped it away.

"I'm fine. Don't touch."

Pete held respectfully back, allowing them to climb past, before bringing up the rear.

The ladder took them to the lower maintenance-levels. They could feel the grind of heavy machinery.

There wasn't much time – they had seen the nuke brought onboard.

"What's the plan?" Mark asked.

Tom whistled speculatively.

"Well, I guess we find the main pipeline and break it somehow."

"They still have the nuke," Pete asked. "What if they blow it up here?"

"They were drilling for a reason," Tom said. "Whatever spot they're aiming for is down deep. I'm guessing far enough that a bomb on the surface won't trigger it.

"Although," he amended quickly, "it'll cook *us* pretty good, so let's not do that either."

Mark smiled fatalistically.

"We're already cooked," he said. "At this point, the best we can do is sabotage the rig before they kill us."

Mark glanced back at Sabrina and Lily.

"These are *your* friends."

He turned on his heel, back towards the main building. He peered in cautiously, as the others gathered behind him.

The hallway inside *looked* clear.

Unfortunately, that meant every sickle-claw on the rig was flocked around the main pipeline and its cargo. Against Pete and Mark's knives.

Tom pointed to the wall where there was a fire-hose, complete with an ax, sitting there handy. Mark shrugged and broke the glass.

An alarm immediately sounded, clanging through the narrow metal halls.

"Awww *shit*," they all said together.

Already they could hear the hooting of sickle-claws, bizarrely reminiscent of barking hounds and cawing crows, echoing down the hall.

Pete and Mark stood in front of the others – Mark wielded the ax. Lily and Sabrina clung to each other, falling back.

But Tom pulled the fire-hose out of the wall, waving Pete and Mark aside as the first of the dromaeosaurs burst into the chamber.

Tom blasted it with a stream of high-pressure water, knocking it down. The moment it hit the floor, Mark chopped its head like a turkey, leaving the body to kick and twitch.

Tom turned the hose down the hallway, pushing the crowding dromaeosaurs back. In the close quarters, the force was overpowering, leaving them tripping and falling over each other.

A pair of stubborn individuals managed to fight their way through, staggered and off-balance — Mark quickly relieved them of their heads.

Pete pushed the chamber door shut, as Tom turned off the hose.

Mark wiped the blood off his ax.

"Find another way up, I guess."

"No," Tom said. "It's pointless. They'll kill us. We'll never get near the main drill."

"But," he added, "we're on the maintenance-level. If we cut the power to the rig..." He shrugged. "That *should* work."

"Better than charging face-first into a troop of sickle-claws," Mark allowed. He tossed the ax over his shoulder, turning back the way they had come. It wasn't impossible. If they could find something as simple as a circuit-breaker, that might at least trip the operation up.

It was obvious why Megs had been in the area, now — the north Pacific coast was pliosaur-territory. Just like the *T. rex* in the Valley, Otto couldn't get past them. The Megs were guard-dogs.

But Megs tended to come up south against pliosaurs.

That was why the Food of the Gods had been added.

Megs also tended to perform better strategically when Otto was around.

Right now it was about stalling. Tom didn't believe the rig would survive the battle. It had already been hit several times. If they had still been outside, they would have already been killed.

Grim options, Tom thought – delay a nuke long enough to be crushed in general crash-and-mash destruction. A nuke would probably hurt less.

But they didn't know it was *truly* hopeless until they opened the doorway to the maintenance-level, to find an entire troop of sickle-claws waiting, with Ottos sitting on their shoulders.

One of them spoke in Tom's voice – a sentence he'd uttered only minutes ago.

"It *should* work."

And then, in all their voices together.

"Awww *shit!*"

Mark slammed the door back shut, even as the sickle-claws charged. It latched a moment before the door was hit from the other side, jarring it on its hinges.

It didn't matter. All they had to do was turn the knob. It wouldn't take long for them to figure *that* out.

"We," Mark announced, "are screwed."

Tom had no ready answer. Pete cursed softly.

Lily and Sabrina looked back at the others apologetically.

Mark regarded the two of them.

"Well," he said, eyeing Lily before turning to

Sabrina, "since we might not have a chance to do this later, is this my daughter?"

There was a heartbeat of silence. Sabrina stared back.

Lily started to speak.

But then the rig was hit again – hard this time – and the floor beneath their feet skewed sharply to one side – a strut had been torn away.

Water began pouring in.

CHAPTER 13

The giant pliosaur came up under the rig, spreading hundred-and-fifty-foot jaws, before clamping down, crumpling the lower deck like paper.

From inside, they saw twelve-foot teeth pierce the frail-steel walls, immediately followed by a deluge of incoming ocean, as the pliosaur cinched its hold and began shaking the entire rig.

"Hang on!" Tom shouted, but the floor was now slanted forty-five degrees, and he found himself sliding towards the rising water.

Lily and Sabrina screamed as they both slipped and fell. Mark threw himself to the floor, grabbing their hands.

Tom caught Pete's grip as he slid past. For an agonizingly long moment, they all perched above the foaming brine.

Then the rig was hit again – it was being attacked from multiple angles now. The pliosaurs had breached the Meg's defenses.

There was a horrible, metallic shriek as the main pipeline, threaded through the center of the rig, piercing down into the crater, was torn open.

This was followed immediately by several successively louder explosions, and then suddenly everything around them was on fire, even the ocean, as it came rushing in.

"Well," Tom said, "at least that nuke hasn't

gone off."

Mark was not comforted.

"Yet," he said.

The rig was hit again, several times in succession. The facility was roughly five times the size of the death-ship, so it took a little longer, with a couple extra sets of jaws, but now the entire rig was being dragged down.

Lily and Sabrina screamed, and Tom heard blue curses from Mark and Pete as they were all pulled under.

The rig itself was torn apart, and open ocean flowed in.

Tom reflexively grabbed a breath, an instinctual survival mechanism – he had a couple of minutes at best and then he would drown.

Maybe not even that long, because something struck his head and he blacked-out.

When he blinked awake, he was disoriented, still reflexively holding his breath – and not much left of it – floating in the dark like he had in orbit.

His head was still throbbing from impact, and the dying air in his lungs spurred apathy instead of activity, as he started to fade from consciousness once again.

Then he was aware of a large black shape rising from below.

He could see two white patches like eyes.

A second later, it was upon him, like a surfacing submarine, and Tom found himself once more clinging to the black dorsal fin of an orca – the resident-matriarch – taking him to the surface.

He gasped air as his head broke water. There was a complimentary burst of vapor from the whale's spout, as the big female circled rapidly away from the demolished and sinking rig.

The rest of the pod surfaced around them. Tom saw Mark and Pete, each clinging to a tall black dorsal. The transient-matriarch carried both Lily and Sabrina.

Behind them, the ocean burned, and the remaining machinery began to explode.

The giant pliosaurs continued to tear at the wreckage. Tom didn't see any more circling Megs, but the pliosaurs' green glowing eyes signified the Food of the Gods was nearing the peak of its cycle – it would not be long before these giant reptilian sea-monsters adapted the knee-jerk aggression of rabid-dogs.

Were these orcas going to carry them all the way back to the coast?

Then, off in the distance, he heard the buzz of rotor-blades.

He spotted a pair of choppers headed their way.

Tom glanced over at Mark, who smiled back.

"Holy shit," Pete hollered over. "Are we going to live?"

"Don't jinx it," Mark called back.

But even now, the choppers turned in their direction. The orca pod seemed to recognize it, veering to meet them.

One of the choppers circled off towards the wreckage, where the pliosaurs were tossing bits of Megalodon meat up in the air, snapping up the pieces like crocs tearing at a hippo carcass.

They also seemed to be slapping repeatedly at the water itself. Tom realized the entire area must be flooded with scrambling sickle-claws – and of course, Otto.

Another thing Tom had noticed about *T. rex* –

they *always* hated Otto, but with infected-giants, it got worse.

These pliosaurs seemed to be responding the same way. That was what they were swatting at. They were going after every last one of the little bastards.

The second chopper circled above them. The side-door opened and Tom saw a man with a rifle start picking shots at the big reptiles. Each shot sounded with a soft *phut*.

Darts. They were administering the antidote to the Food of the Gods.

Directly injected, the effect was immediate – the glowing green faded from their eyes.

Tom waved at the chopper circling above – Maverick and Cameron.

Maverick had brought the cargo chopper, anticipating rescuing a party of eleven. He hovered the bulky old aircraft close to the water, in the path of Tom and his matriarch-orca mount.

They dangled a rope-ladder and the big orca lurched forward, rising up high enough for Tom to grab the rungs. Then she dropped back into the sea and disappeared.

As Tom scrambled up to the waiting chopper, all three orcas followed in succession, handing off their human riders, and then diving straight down out of sight. Behind them, the rest of the pod sounded as well.

"Friends of yours?" Cameron asked as he grabbed Tom's hand, pulling them onboard.

"They are now," Tom replied.

Pete was next, then he and Tom both reached after Sabrina.

"You okay?" Pete asked, helping her onboard.

"I'm fine," Sabrina replied tersely, pulling her hand away, her eyes turning furtively to Cameron and then Maverick in the pilot's seat.

"Well, look who we have here," Maverick offered. "Right in the middle of a shit-storm. *Again.*"

Sabrina frowned, saying nothing, moving quickly aside, making way for Lily. Cameron gave her an up-and-down as well, as he pulled her up onboard. Lily simply shuffled meekly back next to Sabrina.

"I've got to hear *this* story," Cameron said, as he extended his hand to Mark, bringing up the rear.

Mark regarded the two women, his face pole-axed,

"I'm still not quite sure what it is myself," he said.

The second chopper was still circling, firing darts down at the churning water. Maverick touched the radio.

"Hey, fellas," he said, "I'm taking our people home. You gonna be alright?"

"We'll be fine," came the reply. "They're the ones flying with you."

"Smart-ass," Maverick offered back. "See ya back home."

As he tapped the radio off, he dipped the chopper wildly, throwing everyone to one side. He over-corrected, throwing everyone back, before straightening the bird back out again.

Cameron eyed them all meaningfully, as he belted himself into his seat.

There was a brief rush of movement as the others did likewise.

"Seriously," Tom said, as he clung to his seat,

"do you want me to fly?"

"Just hang on," Maverick replied. "We won *our* fight an hour ago. I already started drinkin'."

He danced the chopper a little more just for emphasis, and Tom dutifully shut up.

The helicopter rose in altitude, leaving the wreck-site behind. Ten minutes later, the second chopper followed.

Behind them, the band of pliosaurs was breaking-up too, gulping down the last chunks of Megalodon, and having squashed every last Otto and sickle-claw that still swam or floated.

Presently, they disappeared as well.

It was not long after that, when the pod of orcas appeared once again, at a distance now, circling the site.

And this time, they were accompanied by another boat – a smaller sailboat, guided by the lean figure of a man, white-haired and bearded.

The man put a spyglass to his eye, scoping the burning wreck. Then he turned it to the retreating choppers, heading home for the Valley.

He smiled, turning to the gathered orcas circling his boat.

"Okay, guys," he said, "nice work. Now, let's go home."

CHAPTER 14

Shanna would have gone on the rescue except that immediately on the heels of the battle in the Valley, the first of their expectant mothers had come to term.

As it turned out, Shanna bet wrong – it was not Leanne but Queenie. The giant rex female had probably been killing carcharodonts with labor pains.

It was an unprecedented event in many ways – the first natural birth of a giant, and Shanna wasn't sure what to expect.

Big Red, still with Giganotosaurus blood slathered across his lips, sat at poised attention as his mate curled in her nest – a grove of trees stamped into a circular bed.

Lucas sat perched on Big Red's shoulder, talking into his ear, keeping him calm while, on the ground, the makeshift vet-crew, Shanna, Kristie, and Leanne, as well as a dubious-looking Rosa, who was the only one with actual medical training, attended to Queenie.

"I'm a *doctor*," Rosa said, "not a dragon-vet."

Shanna wondered if the offspring would survive. In nature, there was a limit to how large eggs could get before their shells became too thick for the hatchlings to break – increasing size by a factor of ten would mean they would have to break the shell for them.

Queenie moaned, a cow-like foghorn, as she

began to lay.

Shanna had done a jury-rigged version of an ultrasound and found three eggs – less than a normal rex-clutch.

Queenie lay her eggs in a semi-circle, each of them over twelve-feet long, and she sat back, nuzzling them with her nose.

Shanna brought a pick-ax, just for the occasion. She struck the first two eggs at their center and they cracked open, both spilling out half-formed, still-born fetuses.

Rosa put a hand to her nose.

"Boy, that's rank."

The third egg, however, appeared viable. Shanna could hear tapping from within. Its occupant wanted out. She swung the pick again, cracking the shell up the side.

"Give us some room," she said quickly – a baby rex was born with teeth, and this hatchling expected to be at least the size of an adult crocodile.

The infant kicked at the shell, breaking it the rest of the way open, and they got their first look.

It sat, head cocked and eyes blinking, its claws picking at clinging bits of shell.

They were not, Shanna realized, the two-fingered hands of a *T. rex*.

Rather, they were the strong, three-taloned claws of a dromaeosaur.

He took after his father.

Shanna had assumed because of the length of the gestation period, the sire was Big Red. She had been wrong. They had never seen the pregnancy cycle of an infected-giant before.

The Dragon Lord had taken Queenie for his

mate before she came to the Valley.

The hatchling perched on its two legs, clearing its throat in a turkey-like gaggle.

"I am Drago," it said.

CHAPTER 15

Lily and Sabrina both sensed the new birth, just as they had the birth of the first Dragon Lord.

When the choppers landed in the Valley, with their little rag-tag group of survivors, the first thing Lily and Sabrina did was run.

Kristie had met Major Tom at Maverick's air-park, with her traditional full-body kiss. Mark found Sally waiting as well, all the way from the coast, nine months pregnant, running and latching onto him, and bursting into tears.

Dawn was with her, Mark's daughter with Sally.

Sabrina stared after her venomously, but Lily took her hand and they quickly stole away.

Lily wanted to be far and gone before Mark turned his attention back to them. Sabrina no doubt had many questions about her father, but they would have to wait.

They couldn't risk encountering Shanna, who was currently occupied with midwifing the birth of the baby dragon.

Shanna would see through her. Lily couldn't allow that.

So she and Sabrina stole the nearest truck. Lily picked up a lot of skills on the street – hot-wiring an ignition was just one. They fled the Valley before Shanna sensed their presence.

For whatever reason, some people were particularly sensitive to her empathic light. Lily was one, Sabrina was another – bright lights in their own right, but grown corrupted and dark.

As they made their way north, Lily wondered if that was why Otto brought them along on their little ocean adventure – not for their thumbs, but as a pair of human familiars, perhaps to help block his own presence from Shanna herself.

Lily glanced at her daughter. They hadn't spoken much since leaving the Valley. Sabrina had not yet asked about her father. Lily supposed she knew enough.

After three days, they pulled up to the same house where they lived the previous year. Lily intended to keep moving north, but she wanted some keepsakes.

As they walked up to the front gate, they found the door ajar.

Lily glanced at Sabrina, and drew the pistol she had discovered in their stolen truck – an old-fashioned *.38* caliber wheel-gun with a box of ammo.

Cautiously, they pushed the door open, and stepped inside.

It was dark – they had been gone less than a week, but the house already smelled empty.

Then Sabrina sucked breath and Lily shrieked as an Otto hopped up on the couch.

The little lizard chittered.

Lily aimed the pistol and fired, blowing the scaly little rat off the back of the davenport like a china-cup, splattering blood across the floor.

Sabrina screamed, starting forward as if she'd shot a dog, but Lily caught her arm. Sabrina stared back, wide-eyed and shocked, but Lily shook her head firmly.

Her daughter was having a hard time with this

part of it. Lily knew she couldn't blame her for what she'd been taught – by her and her 'sisters' – but she could no longer condone it.

"Let's go," Lily said. "Pack what you want. We're leaving."

Sabrina nodded, turning for her old room.

Lily turned to the pantry-closet, where they'd kept supplies.

Nestled among the household chemicals, the cleaners, the bleach, was a little sealed-box – hardly a safe, just a little cooler-style lunch-box.

Inside, was a little vial of liquid, glowing green.

Otto's little stash.

Lily looked at the vial thoughtfully – the amount in the syringe-sized bottle was enough to infect the continent.

Probably best not to leave it lying around. She grabbed the cooler and brought it with her as she called out to her daughter.

"Time to go," she said, climbing in the truck, cranking the ignition. Sabrina tossed her bags in the back and slid in beside her.

Lily pulled out onto the broken, cobbled road.

She wondered if the little lizards would follow.

Or, she thought, would they run, like she was, from that new presence in Shanna's Valley?

That was something neither had spoken of yet, either.

Instead, they sat in silence, only hoping they could leave it all behind.

CHAPTER 16

Back at the wreck-site, the ocean burned.

Among the twisted and broken metal was Otto's bomb – a handcrafted little firecracker, that probably would have gone off with fifty-times Hiroshima had it been successfully activated. Now, it was a broken piece of equipment, leaking plutonium into the surrounding water as it sunk into the abyss – a freshly drilled tunnel broken through sixty-five million years of fossilized sediment and rock.

And approximately twenty miles below, past the deepest sea-floor, where the outer crust of the Earth broke through into magma, something stirred.

There was a rumble, as if from a giant growling in his sleep.

And beating in rhythm with the volcanic drum of the planet itself, came a steady, seismic pulse...

... like the heartbeat of something alive.

THE END

Check out other great

Dinosaur Thrillers!

Gustavo Bondoni

TEST SITE HORROR

Lieutenant Max Alexeyev is a Russian Special Forces soldier. His job is to protect his country's interests at home and abroad, not to rescue overly ambitious reporters who have bitten off stories too big to chew. But when his unit gets called to a press event at a laboratory that has been invaded by dinosaurs, that's exactly what he finds himself doing. Fighting both prehistoric nightmares and the products of modern genetic experiments in the forests of the Ural Mountains, he battles for his own survival as well as that of alluring journalist Marianne Caruso and her peers.Unbeknownst to him, however, shadowy human forces are at work to ensure that no one spills the secrets of the research being done in the area.Will they live to tell the story of the Test Site Horror?

John Lee Schneider

AGE OF MONSTERS

Once upon a time, Dinosaurs ruled the Earth.But the Mesozoic era — the Age of Reptiles — came to its cataclysmic end sixty-five million years ago.The Age of Monsters begins tonight.And the world of humankind will crumble. Some will call it Judgment. Some will attempt to fight. Others will simply run. Most will just try and survive. But no one will escape.In the mountains. In the oceans. In the cities and towns. Even up in space.Where were YOU when the world ended?

 SEVERED PRESS

Check out other great

Dinosaur Thrillers!

Doug Goodman

HUNTING WITH DINOSAURS

A hunting party is sent to catch and kill raptors that have escaped Dinosaur Falls Restricted Area and murdered nearby hikers. But the hunters find the raptors are unlike any creature they've ever hunted, and soon one lone bowhunter is running for his life through the Perdidos Mountains. He discovers an old wilderness survival trench and burrows in deep, but eventually the raptors come for him. His only salvation is to befriend a wolf hellbent on destroying the raptors. If they can come together, they can form a pack the world has never seen, but if they fail, the raptors are waiting with their sharp teeth and elongated claws...

Edward J. McFadden III

DINOSAUR RED

There's a doorway on Mars that has mankind's greatest minds perplexed. Deep beneath Aeolis Mons an ancient secret is revealed, and a team of explorers led by Forest Judge, Deputy Commander of Gale Base Alpha, are dispatched to investigate. The prehistoric gateway reveals a biosphere preserving Earth's distant past, and as Judge and crew stand on the threshold of mankind's greatest discovery the Martian ground trembles. A roar thunders from within, the doorway closes, and the team is trapped. Six mission specialists, each with unique skills, each with different reasons for wanting to break free of the primordial trap. To get home Judge is forced to choose between escape and changing the course of humanity. What will he do?

Made in United States
North Haven, CT
03 May 2024

52080668R00078